THE
GOOD
NEIGHBORS
KIERSTEN MODGLIN

www.kierstenmodglinauthor.com
Cover Design: Tadpole Designs
Editing: Three Owls Editing
Formatting: Tadpole Designs
First Print Edition: 2019
First Electronic Edition: 2019

PRAISE FOR THE GOOD NEIGHBORS

The twists and turns Modglin is known for will have you on the edge of your seat in this *unputdownable* story about neighbors and the secrets they keep.

RACHEL RENEE, AUTHOR OF *THE SAVANNAH PD SERIES*

The Supreme Queen of Twists, Kiersten Modglin, has done it again!

MANDY, JANISE'S JIVIN' BOOK BLOG

The plot twists kept me on the edge of my seat, up until the early morning, flipping the pages. I needed answers, and when they were exposed, I was not left disappointed.

KATE BLANCHARD, AUTHOR OF *DEAR ANNA*

Ms. Modglin adds a dramatic, eerie twist...

J. LYNN LOMBARD, AUTHOR OF *THE RACING DIRTY SERIES*

[The Good Neighbors] is a true must read!

ANNAMARIE GARDNER, AUTHOR OF *YOUNG FAE*

…suspenseful and exciting and mind blowing!

What a wonderfully woven web Modglin made, as has come to be her trademark style, and all becomes clear at the end. Addictive, unsettling, intriguing, shocking, and just as the book promises about the neighbors, there is much more to this well-written story than first meets the eye.

To my dad—
For always being on my side, making me laugh no matter how mad
I am, and teaching me that the best neighbor is no neighbor at all.

CHAPTER ONE

HARPER

Harper sank down in the back of the U-Haul, wiping the sweat from her brow with a heavy sigh.

"That's it," she told her husband as he walked out onto their new front porch. "That's the last of it."

He nodded, hopping down from the porch and bounding up the metal ramp of the truck at breakneck speed. "Whatsa matter, wimp?" he teased, elbowing her.

She took a deep breath, rolling her eyes at him. "Dude, I am not used to this humidity. How are you not dying?"

He laughed. "You do know I'm from Florida, right?"

"You haven't lived there in years."

"Still. You don't forget heat like this. Southern heat is all the same," he said simply. "Here, let's get you inside, and we'll cool off." He stood, lifting and carrying his wife like a doll. Their skin stuck together from the heat, but she couldn't help tossing her head back with a loud laugh. He stopped as they hit the ramp to exit the truck, staring off into the distance.

"What's wrong?" Harper asked, looking his way before

following his gaze to the house next door. The two-story white house stood a few feet from theirs, perfect black shutters and a white picket fence making it picturesque. It could have come from a magazine. In fact, she realized the longer she stared, so could the couple standing on its porch.

Tall and lean, even from a distance their beauty was breathtaking. The woman, perhaps a few years older than Harper and Bryant, had stick straight, platinum blonde hair and a perfect figure. Her white suit was neatly pressed, and if she hadn't just walked out onto the porch, Harper would've thought she was a mannequin. Her shoulders were perfectly squared, her posture enviable. She was *perfect.* As was the man standing next to her—his raven black hair sat thick atop his head, his high cheekbones and muscled body making him an exquisite companion to the woman whose arm was wrapped through his.

Snapping out of her stupor, Harper stuck her hand over her head, waving wildly. "Hello," she called, feeling idiotic when they remained still.

As her hand slid back down, she looked over to her husband, who seemed equally in awe of their model-like neighbors. When she looked back, the woman had leaned her head over toward the man's ear, whispering something to him.

Their stony expressions did not change as they turned around, not waving or even offering a smile to their new neighbors, and headed back into their house.

"Jeez, tough crowd," Bryant whispered, setting her down and closing the door to the U-Haul.

"That was weird, right?"

"Very weird," he agreed.

"I thought people in the South were supposed to be nicer," she said softly.

"Nah, they just put that on the brochures," he teased, scooping her back up again and darting for the house. She let out another loud laugh, kissing him quickly and forgetting, at least for the moment, about their strange welcome.

HARPER

"Have you seen my gray pajama pants?" Harper yelled through the house, trying to make sure he could hear her over the running water in the kitchen.

The water shut off, and she heard his footsteps coming toward her. "I think they were in one of the boxes in the spare bedroom."

She nodded, zigzagging in between boxes on her way toward the spare room. It had been three days since they'd moved in, and still everything in the house was chaotic. Harper didn't like disorder. If it were up to her, they would've stayed up all night getting everything unpacked and put away. Only then would she feel at peace.

Bryant was the opposite. He could live out of boxes for weeks. He'd proven that fact when he'd moved in with her their senior year of college. It had taken him forever to finally get his stuff unpacked. In fact, once he had, it had only been a few months before they had to repack to move out of that compact apartment and into their home in the city.

Then, a few months after their wedding, he'd gotten a job offer in Lancaster Mills, and they'd headed south to settle down. Harper could be happy here. She really could. *If only they could get these damn boxes unpacked before they had gray hair.*

Interrupting her thoughts, the doorbell rang, and she sprinted back into the living room just as Bryant was opening the door. She stopped short when she saw who was waiting. The couple from next door…Mr. and Mrs. Model.

"Um, hello," Bryant said, his smile much too wide for Harper's taste. She couldn't be mad at him, though, as she felt her own smile lighting up as the woman met her eyes.

Up close, they were even more beautiful than she'd imagined. Gorgeous, porcelain skin and smooth, unwavering hair even in the humid North Carolina summer. The woman smiled at her, her teeth so white it had to be unnatural, but behind full, red lips they seemed to fit perfectly. There was that word again. *Perfect.* It was the only word Harper could summon to describe the couple.

"Hey," the woman said with a soft tone, her words like butter. "I'm Tori. This is my husband, Jason." She smiled again, holding out a hand which Bryant quickly took. "We're your new neighbors."

Jason held out his hand to Harper, shaking it quickly. "I'm Harper," she said. "And this is my husband, Bryant."

Bryant stepped back, holding out his arm. "Would you like to come in?"

"Oh, we'd hate to impose," the woman said, though she continued to wait for a further invitation.

"It's no trouble," Harper assured her.

"Just excuse our mess," Bryant said, shutting the heavy wooden door behind them after they entered.

Harper forced herself not to roll her eyes. *Our mess. The one he'd refused to help with an hour ago.*

"Oh, don't be silly," Jason said, his voice deeper, fuller than she'd imagined. "Our house looks like this all the time."

"Well, it did," Tori corrected him, "until we got a house-keeper. She's great, really. I can give you her number."

Harper nodded. "Thank you. We might take you up on that once we get unpacked. A house this big, I'm not sure what we're going to do with it."

"It really is lovely," Tori said, admiring the space that Harper was, in fact, proud of. It was the nicest place they'd ever owned, and even though there were updates they planned to do, for now, it was pretty great.

"We've never had anything this nice. We're used to apartments, so this place is practically a castle. Of course, it's nothing compared to your house."

"Yes, well, we have a bit *too much* space if you ask me," Tori said, smirking slightly. "You two are from the city, right? Up north?"

"Chicago," Bryant answered.

"Really?" Tori patted her husband's shoulder. "Jason does work there all the time."

"You do?" Harper gasped, happy to hear about home in any way.

"I mean, I wouldn't say *all the time*," he told her, "but a fair bit, yeah."

"Really?" Bryant asked. "What do you do?"

"I'm a writer. Mostly freelance sports stuff, but I do whatever they pay me for."

"Whoa, that's really incredible."

"Yeah, well, living the dream, right?" he said with a small laugh. "Paid to travel, amazing job, gorgeous wife." He wrapped an arm around her waist. "What about you guys? What do you do?"

"Oh, um, I'm a history teacher," Bryant said. "I just got a job at the high school here. Living the dream too, right?" He pulled Harper to his side, and she couldn't help but tense up. What was it about this couple that made her so on edge?

"And you?" Jason asked, looking at her now, his intense gaze causing her to blush.

"I'm, um, I...well, I work at the hospital."

"You do?" Tori spoke up, staring at her intently. "I guess we'll be seeing each other around, then. I'm a plastic surgeon." *Of course.* "What do you do?"

"Reception," Harper answered, her voice squeaking slightly. She had no reason to feel ashamed of her job. She'd gone to college and gotten her degree in healthcare administration. Now it was just a matter of working her way up. She couldn't help it that her husband's first job offer came from a podunk town whose closest hospital was over a half-hour from their new home.

"Oh, well that's okay," Tori said, her tone patronizing as if she were talking to a child.

"I know it is," Harper said with a stiff nod.

"Well, anyway," Jason spoke up, easing the tension. "We wanted to say welcome to the neighborhood. We felt silly coming over without any wine or baked goods or something...so we wanted to see if you two would like to join us for dinner tomorrow night? Our place."

"Oh, I don't—" Harper started to object.

"We won't take no for an answer," Jason told her, a small smile on his lips.

She sighed, her body coursing with adrenaline, and she forced herself to look away. "Okay, sure."

"Really?" Tori clapped her hands together in front of her chest. "Oh, great. What do you like? We can do anything. We'll be ordering out, of course. These hands," she held up her perfectly manicured hands, "may be able to do a perfect skin graft, but they can burn water, I swear." She laughed, flipping her long, blonde hair over her shoulder.

"Oh, we aren't picky. Tacos, pizza, whatever," Bryant said.

Tori's mouth twisted. "Oh, okay. Sure...we can do...*tacos*

or pizza." She looked at Jason as if they'd suggested they eat buckets of lard for dinner.

"We aren't picky, like he said. Just...surprise us with whatever you like," Harper offered.

She clasped her hands in front of her chest. "Beautiful. We'll do that. Come on over around seven, okay?" Tori asked, but without waiting for an answer, she grabbed Jason's hand and pulled him toward the door. "We'll be going. Sorry to have bothered you all. We're looking forward to tomorrow."

"Us too," Bryant said. "I'm really glad you guys came over. We thought you must've hated us after the other day."

Harper furrowed her brow at her husband, closing her eyes to hide the fact that they were rolling. Tori and Jason stopped in their tracks, the room seeming to chill over as they turned around. "The other day?" Tori asked, her voice an octave higher.

"Yeah," Bryant said, oblivious to any awkwardness. "When we moved in. We waved at you, but you didn't seem too happy to see us move in. We thought you guys must've been total assholes." He slapped Jason's shoulder, letting out a laugh.

"I don't know what you're talking about," Tori said firmly, her lips pressed into a thin line.

Bryant moved his hand back from Jason's shoulder, staring at them. Finally, the gravity of the situation had sunk in, and he seemed to realize what he'd done. "You know what, with the distance between us...we probably couldn't even see your face that well. You were probably not looking our way."

Jason nodded, a forced smile on his face. "That must be it."

"If we'd seen you, of course we would've come and said hello. What kind of neighbors would we be if we didn't?"

Tori asked, a hand to her chest. "I'm sorry if there was any confusion."

Bryant nodded, his shoulders relaxing. "Of course. Sorry about that."

"Right. Well, no bother. We'll see you tomorrow?" Tori asked, opening the door.

"See you tomorrow," Harper told her, watching as her husband shut the door behind them and letting out a deep breath she hadn't realized she'd been holding.

What the hell just happened?

CHAPTER THREE

HARPER

The next night, the couple paced the house just before seven. "Why did we agree to this again?"

"Relax," Bryant said, grasping her shoulders and moving a piece of hair from her eyes. "Everything's going to be fine. Besides, it'll be nice to make a few friends here. Get to know some other people. Why are you so worried?"

"Because, Bryant, we're not *couple-friend* people. And even if we were, they're just…strange, don't you think?"

"It was weird last night, right?" he confirmed, and she let out a breath, glad it wasn't just her that noticed.

"I mean, yeah. Super weird."

He let go of her shoulders, looking away. "Okay, well, it's already nearly time to be there. We can't flake out now. So, let's go and get it over with, and then from now on we'll avoid going there until they get the hint. I don't want to make them think we don't like them. That would make it even worse, and they're going to be our neighbors for the foreseeable future. We don't want to make things more awkward."

Harper sucked in a breath. "You're right. I'm sorry, I don't know why I'm so worried about this."

He kissed her forehead. "Don't worry about it. We're in a new place surrounded by new people. You're probably just homesick." He grabbed the wine from the shelf by the stairs and pulled open the door. "Come on now," he said, patting her bottom as she walked past him.

They walked down their porch stairs and across the large front yard. Harper looked up at the sky, taking in a deep breath. "You don't see nights like this in Chicago, that's for sure."

He wrapped an arm around her shoulders. "It's beautiful, isn't it? I didn't realize how much I missed the stars."

She smiled, pulling his arm down so they were holding hands. She had to admit, the neighborhood *was* beautiful. Their house sat at the end of a subdivision with few houses around them. In fact, other than Tori and Jason's, the next nearest house was at the end of the block. The paved streets were well maintained, and there were pruned trees lining each driveway.

She should feel comfortable, she knew. There were people who would love to have this much space. This much space in Chicago would've cost a fortune. They'd gotten the house for a steal here, way below market value, and it had been a no-brainer. But, she didn't feel comfortable yet. Harper had always been a city girl. She felt safe there. She could breathe when there was no room to breathe. Somehow, here with all the air in the world, she felt suffocated.

Before she could dwell on it too much, they'd made it across their lawn and were walking up the short drive to the white house. The front porch was quaint—more beautiful up close, much like its inhabitants—with two white rocking chairs and cute, red cushions filling their seats. In between the chairs sat a white wicker table with an antique watering can. The house *literally* could've come from a magazine.

Bryant released her hand before knocking on the door, and the porch light flicked on in an instant. The solid black door, its beveled glass window at the top, opened quickly, and Jason stood in front of them.

"Hey guys," he greeted them warmly, holding out a hand to shake Bryant's as if they were old friends. He ushered them into the elegant living room, shutting the door behind them. "Welcome! Come on in. Make yourselves at home."

Harper took in the home: its large fireplace with distressed-wood mantel; the black, leather sectional and recliner that looked as if they had been shipped in just that day; the large, flat screen television that adorned the wall. Their home was, of course, perfect, and Harper let out a gasp before she realized it had happened.

"Yeah," Jason said. "Perks of marrying a doctor, right?" He placed his hands in his pockets, shrugging.

Harper nodded, her lips pressed together. "It's beautiful."

"Thanks," he said simply. "Hey, what can I get you guys to drink? We've got everything...beer, wine—red and white—sparkling water, *and* sweet tea. We *are* Southern, after all. What will it be?"

"Oh, um, white wine will be fine," Harper said politely.

"Beer for me," Bryant answered. "Man, what size is that TV?"

"Uh, I think it's like ninety inches or something," Jason said with a laugh. "You guys come on in here," he told them as he made his way into the kitchen. "Tori will be down any minute, and then we can eat."

"It smells amazing," Bryant told him as they made their way into the equally breathtaking kitchen. Brass fixtures and black and white marble countertops—*of course, it was gorgeous.*

"Oh, well, we can't take credit for it. I hope you guys like ribeyes. We order from this great little place across town. The best steak you'll ever eat."

"Oh, man, that sounds amazing," Bryant said happily. Harper couldn't help noticing how eager to please their new neighbors he was.

"I was thinking we could eat on the patio tonight." Tori's voice came from behind them. Harper spun around to see their host. She was dressed in a plain, black, off-the-shoulder jumpsuit, her white-blonde hair slicked back, lips pale in comparison to her dark eye makeup. She looked very New York to be from such a small town.

"Oh, okay," Jason said, quickly gathering the plates from the table. "That sounds great." Why was he equally as eager to please his wife? Harper guessed when you had a wife that looked like Tori, you would be.

They followed Tori out the back set of French doors and onto a patio lit by tiki torches and took a seat at the table waiting for them. Jason set the plates down, hurrying back inside and returning moments later with their food and drinks.

"Wow, this looks delicious," Harper said, and she really meant it. She waited for someone else to begin eating—*of course it was Bryant*—before she picked up her fork.

"So, Harper, you said you work at the hospital. Have they given you a shift yet?" Tori asked, taking the tiniest bite Harper had ever seen.

"Yeah, I'm swinging between firsts and seconds for a while."

"Oh, rough," Tori said, pushing her lips to one side of her mouth. "You know, Randall owes me a favor. I could see about pulling some strings to get you on days permanently if you want."

"Oh, no, that's okay," Harper told her, probably too quickly. "Honestly, I don't mind."

"You are a better woman than me. I couldn't handle it. I need my beauty sleep," Tori said with a laugh.

"Really? I wouldn't think as a surgeon you would get much sleep."

"Oh, I don't work at the hospital," she said, chewing up a bit of food before she finished her sentence. "No, I own my own clinic. It's just across the street, though I do get called in for consults from time to time. So, I'm sure you'll see me around." She smiled. "It's nice to have a friend when you're someplace new."

Harper smiled, trying to read her expression, though for the first time it seemed genuine. "Are you both from here?" she asked. Tori looked at Jason, their faces growing somewhat bleak. "Oh, I'm sorry. That's none of my business, honestly."

"No," Tori said, looking back her way and placing her fork down. "It's okay. Really, it is. It's just...it's a tough subject, you know? Jay and I...well, he grew up in Tennessee. I was a foster child. I'd bounced around from home to home until his family took me in when I was sixteen." She reached across the table and squeezed his hand. "So, to answer your question, no we're not from here, but I moved around so much as a kid I never really know what to say when I'm asked where it is I'm from."

"Oh my god, I'm so sorry," Harper told her, her face growing warm from embarrassment. *Foster siblings that had gotten married?* Was that even allowed? It seemed odd, but she had no time to dwell on it because Tori was talking again, interrupting her thoughts.

"No, there's no need to be. Honestly," Tori let go of her husband's hand and reached for Harper's, "it's okay. It was a long time ago, and you couldn't have known. Besides, my story has a happy ending. That's all that really matters."

Harper nodded, feeling awkward as Tori held her hand for a bit longer. When she finally released it, but before Harper could look away, she noticed Tori wiping a tear from the corner of her eye. She took a deep breath, realizing she'd been caught.

"Sorry. It's...old memories." She tried to laugh through her tears as she stood from the table. "Excuse me for just a minute."

"Of course—" Harper said, though it fell on deaf ears as Tori was already back inside before she'd finished speaking. "I'm so sorry. I feel awful," she told Jason before looking at her husband who looked equally mortified.

"Don't be," he said. "Tori...she seems cold, I know, but she's had a rough go of things. Her childhood was really bad. She doesn't like to talk about it. Even *I* don't know everything." He paused, taking a breath. "Look, I know it's an awkward situation, but she's not mad at you. You couldn't have known. She just gets upset thinking of all she's gone through. I guess what I'm saying is, please don't write her off. She could use a friend. Someone normal. She's surrounded by all those stuffy doctors at work and...well, she's never really been the type to have friends. People aren't open to her." He shrugged. "I don't mean to seem crass, but when you look like Tori does, people assume you're, well, to be frank, a bitch. Excuse the French. But, if they'd give her a chance, they'd see the side of her I see. She's one of the most genuine people I've ever met."

Harper nodded, unsure of what to say. Not an hour ago, she'd been one of those people. Judging her neighbor based solely on her looks and the awkward first encounter. Maybe Bryant was right, maybe they really *hadn't* seen them. Perhaps she'd judged them too harshly. After all, they had invited them to dinner to welcome them to the neighborhood. She let her shoulders slump, feeling even worse.

"Maybe I should go check on her?" she asked.

"She'll be back," Jason said. "She's resilient, my wife. Beautiful and strong as they come."

As if on command, the door opened, and Tori stood in front of them with a new bottle of wine. "Sorry about that. Who needs a refill?"

Harper lifted her glass in an instant, trying to make amends for the awkwardness her innocent question had brought to their evening, yet knowing no amount of wine could erase the guilt that was eating her from the inside out.

CHAPTER FOUR

HARPER

Three days into her first week at Crittenden Hospital, Harper was finally starting to get the hang of her new environment. She had settled in nicely to her new workspace, making friends with the coworkers, and though she was still constantly asked where she was from and why her accent was so weird, she was starting to feel more comfortable with each passing day.

She checked her phone for the second time, waiting to see if Bryant had ever messaged her to tell her what to pick up for dinner. He was supposed to be deciding, but the man treated even the most simple decisions as if they were life and death. She groaned at seeing the blank screen and slipped it back into her pocket.

"Hey," Devon said, startling her. Her coworker rolled his chair next to hers. "You wanna grab a drink tonight?"

She furrowed her brow. It was totally out of the blue. "You know I'm married, right?"

"Yeah, I noticed," he said, pointing to her ring. "It's not a date...just a work thing. All of us are going." He gestured toward the four other receptionists, who all nodded in agreement despite being tied up with patients. "We try to get together once a month and grab a drink or whatever. But, if you're not up for it—"

"No," she said quickly. "No, I'm up for it. Where are we going?"

"Nice," he said, biting his lip and nodding. "It's a little bar downtown called Sam's."

"You'll love it, Harper," Collette whispered, covering the phone's mouthpiece with her well-manicured hand.

"Okay, cool. Are we meeting there?"

"Yeah, we'll just head out after work. You can follow me," he told her, sliding back over to assist a nurse.

Harper pulled out her phone once again, typing out a quick text.

Nevermind. I'm going to go out with a few friends for drinks after work. Won't be too late. Love you.

She watched the screen as the little bubbles popped across, indicating that he was typing a message.

After a few moments, his message came through. **That's fine. I'll reheat leftovers. Be careful. I'll see you tonight.**

She sent a heart emoji, trying to make sure he was okay with her impromptu plans, and he reciprocated. *Easy enough. Maybe things really would be different here.*

CHAPTER FIVE

HARPER

Later that evening at Sam's, Harper was feeling herself sliding a bit closer to her new normal. The group of people she worked with—Devon, Collette, Miranda, Savannah, and James—was down to earth and a lot of fun.

Miranda, with her sleeve full of tattoos she managed to keep hidden at work, slid a glass of beer to Harper.

"Oh, I'm not really a beer drinker," she said softly, hoping she wouldn't offend Miranda.

"You'll like it," Collette insisted. "It's a Lancaster Mills local beer. Strawberry."

"Strawberry beer?" Harper asked, picking up the glass and sniffing it carefully.

"If you don't like it, you don't have to drink it, but at least try it," Miranda insisted.

She pressed the glass to her lips, beginning to take a sip and then choking as she inhaled it involuntarily, shocked at the sight in front of her. She slammed the glass down, clutching her throat as her chest heaved with coughs.

"Jeez, that bad?" Devon asked with a laugh.

"No," she said once her airway was clear. "No, I—" She

looked over, trying to make sense of what she'd seen. It couldn't be, could it? She blinked again, staring at the empty barstool where he'd just been. It must've been someone else. It had to be. But she wouldn't forget those eyes. And his face wasn't exactly common. "I thought I saw someone." She lowered her gaze, feeling her cheeks heat up. "It was actually really good," she assured them, taking another small sip for good measure. It was true. It was decent anyway, for someone who usually hated beer in general.

"Are you stalking me or something?" She heard his voice behind her and shot around. *Okay, so she wasn't crazy.*

"Jason?" she asked, staring at the man with wide eyes. They hadn't seen their neighbors since their dinner over a week ago, but he was pretty unforgettable. She'd known that was him across the room. Him that locked eyes with her as she'd lifted her glass. "What are you doing here?"

"Same thing as you, apparently," he said, lifting his own beer glass. "Unless, of course, you *are* stalking me."

"I'm not stalking you," she said, her face warming even more. She turned to look at her group of friends, the girls at the table staring at him in wonder. "I'm here with friends from work. Collette, Miranda, Savannah, Devon, James," she worked her way around the table, "this is Jason, my neighbor."

An echo of hellos rang out from the table, and Jason nodded his head at them. "Evening, guys," he said, before letting his gaze fall back on her. "You mind if I join you?"

"Not at all!" Savannah squealed before Harper could answer.

"Apparently *not at all*," Harper responded, a small laugh in her voice. Jason pulled up a seat from the table next to them, sliding in beside her so that their arms had no choice but to touch.

"All right, next round's on me," he said, raising his hand so the waiter would notice him.

Cheers were heard all around, and Harper took another drink of her beer, locking eyes with Jason as she swallowed. He lifted his thumb, brushing her upper lip as the room seemed to stand still.

"Bit of foam," he whispered before asking the waiter to bring another round of what everyone was having.

When he wasn't looking, she placed her hand over where his touch had been, feeling silly for the way her heart was racing. Okay, so he was gorgeous...he was also married. *She* was married. Happily married.

She tried to clear her head, thinking more about Bryant. It would've been so much easier if their skin wasn't touching, his body heat transferring to her.

"So, what do you do, Jason?" Miranda asked, taking a shot of vodka as if it were supposed to impress him.

"I'm a writer," he said simply, not bothering to explain it all like he had for Harper.

"That's...romantic," Collette said, leaning forward onto the table as if she were melting.

"Not really," he said. "It's all boring, freelance stuff."

Harper wanted to explain to him that with a face like his, he could literally be writing about sewage and the girls would think it was *romantic,* but she didn't bother. Instead, she scooted a bit closer, tucking a piece of hair behind her ear.

"Jason, you married?" Devon asked, nodding toward his ring. Harper had seen the way Devon flirted with Savannah, and she couldn't help but smile at the obvious jealousy in his voice.

"Yeah," Jason said, lifting his hand up to stare at it. "I sure am."

The girls' spirits visibly fell, though they were lifted again

21

as the waiter approached their table with drinks. Once he'd passed them around and walked away, their small talk filled the quiet.

"So, rough day?" Jason asked, keeping his voice low so the others couldn't hear them well. He was speaking directly to Harper, and somehow that felt intimate.

She shook the thought from her head. It wasn't *supposed* to feel intimate. This was ridiculous. She was like a teenage girl again with all the raging hormones that being thirteen had brought.

"Sorry, what?" she asked, noticing he was still staring, and she'd completely forgotten the question.

"I asked if you'd had a rough day. You know, being here instead of at home."

"Oh, no. Not at all, actually. We just…came here to blow off some steam."

He nodded, downing the last of his beer and beginning to work on the next glass. "Where's Bryant?"

"He's at home. I've put him on unpacking duty."

He laughed.

"What about Tori? Why isn't she here?"

"Ah, Tori," he said with a sigh. "She's…well, it's nearly seven on a Wednesday, so she's probably stopped by the spa to get a massage."

"A massage?"

"She likes to end the day with one," he said with a shrug. "It's her money."

"Must be nice—" She let the thought slip from her head without warning, but Jason didn't seem to mind.

"Yeah, it is." He laughed out loud, and if he weren't so friendly it would've been an obnoxious comment.

"So, what are you doing here, then? You didn't want a massage?" she teased.

"Nah, this is where I come to relax."

"What? That big ole house isn't relaxing enough?"

He shook his head. "Not in the least. I don't think anyone can truly relax in their own home."

"I think ninety-nine percent of the population would disagree with you there," she argued, cocking her head to the side.

"Well, ninety-nine percent of the population doesn't live in my home, then," he said, his eyes growing dark as he stared at her. She knew then that he had a secret—maybe more than one. She leaned closer without thought, as if she were trying to read his thoughts. He stared at her, unblinking, as if he were daring her to try.

"You guys okay?" Collette asked, interrupting her thoughts.

She pulled back, looking down as her face flushed beet red. "Yeah, fine."

"Yep," Jason said. "I'm actually going to head out. My wife will be home any minute. Do you need a ride, Harper?" he asked, touching her shoulder.

She tucked her head over on his hand. "No, thank you. I'll be fine." It was polite. Formal. *Go home.* She was doing the right thing. The bar was dimly lit, she had alcohol in her system. That was the only reason for the sudden tension she felt around him. Tomorrow she'd be back to normal. Everything would be fine, then.

"All right. I'll see you around. Nice to meet you," he said, walking past their table. As he reached the counter, sliding a card to the bartender to pay his tab, he looked back over his shoulder. Their eyes met once again, the heat between them still alive even from several feet away.

Yep, it would definitely be fine tomorrow.

CHAPTER SIX

BRYANT

Bryant sealed the last of the lasagna into the large Tupperware dish, slipping it into the refrigerator quickly before grabbing a beer. He checked the time. It was nearly seven. Surely she'd be home soon.

He wasn't the type of guy to be clingy. He knew it was healthy for Harper to have her own space, but that didn't mean he didn't miss her when she was gone. Especially now, in a new place with no one around. Until the school year started in two weeks, he spent his days unpacking and surfing the internet.

He heard footsteps approaching the door and smiled, taking another sip of his beer and expecting to hear the door open. Instead, he heard a quiet knock. He peered around the corner, watching the door, but without the porch light on he couldn't make out who could be standing there. He set his beer on the counter, walking toward the door cautiously, and flipped on the switch. In the beveled glass, he could see a tall, thin, blonde outline. *Tori.*

He pulled the door open quickly, wondering what on earth she could be doing here so late. "Tori?"

"Hey, Bryant, sorry. I know it's late. Do you…do you mind if I come in?"

He stepped back, his mouth suddenly feeling like cotton. "S-sure. What's up?" he asked. She was dressed in a skintight red dress that left little to the imagination, her hair tied in a loose ponytail at the nape of her neck. "Sorry. I just got home from work, and Jay isn't home. I guess I lost my key somewhere. I just texted him to ask him to come home and let me in. And, well, I was going to sit in my car, but I figured…I could come over and visit you and Harper, if that's okay?"

"Oh, uh, sure. Yeah. Well, Harper's out with friends right now," he said, swallowing hard. "But you're welcome to hang out." He ran his hands through his hair nervously. "Do you want a beer or something?"

"No, I wouldn't want to trouble you."

"It's no trouble," he assured her. "We've got white wine, too."

"Is the beer light?" she asked. "I know, it's stupid, but I'm trying to lose a few pounds." She ran a hand over her tiny waist, her hand moving slowly from hip to hip as if trying to hypnotize him. He looked back up, staring into the kitchen and trying to think of something, *anything*, other than the low-cut neckline on her dress.

"I don't think so. Sorry."

"White wine will be fine, then," she said, taking a step toward the kitchen. "In here?"

He nodded, following her as she led the way through his own house. When they reached the cabinets, he pulled a glass down and filled it a little less than halfway. "It's probably not the kind you like."

She took a sip, her red lips leaving a slight ring around the rim of the glass. "Why do you say that?" she asked, her voice low in her throat.

"Well, I mean, it's not, expensive, or whatever," he said softly, stammering over his words.

"Do you think I'm a snob or something?"

He shook his head. "No, of course not. I'm sorry. I didn't mean that offensively."

"Relax, baby," she told him with a small laugh. She winked, giving him a sultry pout as her free hand traced her neckline absentmindedly. "We're all friends here."

He picked up his beer, taking another drink. "How long do you think Jason will be?" he asked, staring out the window to avoid looking at his guest.

"Oh, he should be home any minute," she said, glancing at her watch. She swallowed the glass of wine quickly, licking her lips and handing it back. Their hands touched briefly as she passed it over, and lightning shot through him at her touch. He turned to the sink, setting the glass in it as her phone beeped.

He felt a hand touch his back, and suddenly her voice was next to his ear. "That's him. Thanks for…taking care of me tonight. I owe you one."

"Anytime." He closed his eyes, staring at her lip print on the glass and listening as her heels clicked slowly across the floor before he heard the door shut. He could still feel her hand on his back, her long nails dragging a slow trail across his skin. He bit his lip, trying to ignore the swelling in his pants. Trying to think of anything besides those red lips, the plunging neckline, her swaying hips. God, what was it about that woman? What was she doing to him?

Without thinking, without allowing himself to think too much about how pathetic he was, he lifted the wine glass from the sink, placing his lips over her lip print and tipping the glass up so the last remaining drop of wine slipped into his mouth.

CHAPTER SEVEN

HARPER

When Harper got home that night, Bryant was already in bed. She tiptoed across the bedroom, sliding out of her scrubs carefully. She noticed the wadded up hand towel on the floor next to the bed, picking it up and tossing it into the hamper.

Guess you got impatient waiting for me.

She grabbed her pajamas from the window seat, throwing them on and walking toward the dresser, then picked up her hairbrush and ran it through her tangled hair.

When she was done, she took off her wedding ring, sliding under the covers and across the bed. He stirred, sucking in a deep breath through his nose and looking at her with one eye open.

"Hey," he said, his voice soft. He looked at the clock on the wall. "You're home late."

"Yeah," she said, running a hand across his chest. "Sorry."

"It's okay," he told her, pressing his dry lips to hers. "You have fun?"

She nodded. "I did, yeah. How was your day?"

"It was good," he said simply, staring at her.

"What's wrong?"

"Nothing." He shook his head, running a hand over his face.

"You sure?"

"Mhm."

"Hey, you'll never guess who I ran into tonight." On the way home, she'd contemplated whether or not to tell him. It wasn't a big deal. She didn't want to make it seem like a big deal, but she also didn't want him to hear about it from Jason and worry she'd been trying to hide it. So, she would tell him. And she would make it seem like it wasn't a big deal.

Because it wasn't.

"Who?" he asked, rolling over so that he was facing her.

"Jason. From next door."

"What? He was at the hospital?"

"No, the bar," she said, trying to read his expression in the moonlight.

"Weird," he said, staring at the wall with a strange expression. "Did he recognize you?"

"Yeah," she admitted. "He came over to say hello." She twisted her mouth. "Tori wasn't with him."

He swallowed. "Hmm."

"It wasn't a big deal, though," she said, kissing him again.

"I didn't say it was," he responded, his voice tense.

"You aren't mad at me, are you? I mean, it's not like I knew he'd be there. I was out with my friends from work. I wouldn't have even said anything to him, but he came over and said hello. It was super brief."

"Whoa, I'm not mad," he told her, squeezing her hand. "Unless I have a reason to be?"

"No. You don't."

He nodded, pulling her onto his chest. "Okay then."

She ran a finger through the hair on his chest. "Did you miss me today?"

"I did. I really, really did," he said. She smiled half-heartedly, though he couldn't see her face. Her mind was drifting elsewhere, but she couldn't help noticing how distant his voice sounded.

———

THE NEXT MORNING, Harper sat at her desk sipping on her mug of coffee while it was still too hot. She was exhausted. She'd spent most of the night tossing and turning, waiting for a reluctant sleep to finally take her.

"What's up, girl?" Collette asked, sliding her chair over to take the station next to her.

"Hey," she said, smiling sleepily at her.

"I had a lot of fun last night. I'm glad you could come."

"Yeah, thanks. I did, too."

"Sam's is pretty cool, huh?"

"Yeah, it was all right."

"So, what's the deal with that guy?" she asked, cutting straight to the chase. Harper had been waiting for the conversation to inevitably steer that way.

"Jason?" She furrowed her brow as if she were confused.

"Of course Jason. He's really married?"

"Yes, he is." The answer came from in front of them, a patient who'd approached Harper's window. She looked up, recognizing the voice but unable to place it until she saw her face.

"Tori, hi," she said, standing up instantly as if she were the damn Queen of England.

Tori's cool glare locked with Collette's. "To answer your question, *again, yes,* Jason is married. To me."

Collette's chair slid away from her, leaving Harper alone. "Nice to meet you," she mumbled when she was further away.

After a moment, Tori's icy, blue-green eyes fell onto Harper once again. "Hey, sorry, I didn't mean to interrupt."

The change in tone was almost scary—her irritated inflection gone, replaced with a friendly smile and cheery stance.

"No, it's fine. Um, is everything okay?" She bit her lip, wondering what, if anything, Jason had told her about the night before. *Not that there was anything to tell.*

"Yeah, of course. I just wanted to stop by. What time do you get off? Four?"

"Mhm," she said, tucking a piece of hair behind her ear.

"Great. Do you want to go to the gym with me after work? I'm *the worst* about going, so I figured having an accountability partner could help."

"Oh, I don't know..." she said, trying to think of a reason, any reason, to say no.

"Please," she stuck out her bottom lip into a pout, "it would really mean a lot to me. I could use a friend who's actually genuine. I feel like we really clicked the other night, don't you?"

She nodded, swallowing. "Yeah, okay. Sure."

Tori squealed, her blonde hair shaking as she lifted up to the balls of her feet in excitement. "Great. I'll come by and we can ride together." She grabbed Harper's hand from the counter, squeezing it carefully. "See you then." With that, she turned, hurrying out of the lobby.

When Harper spun around, every eye in the room was following her friend.

"Who *was* that?" James asked.

"And can she please have my babies?" Devon asked, his face ashen, eyes wide.

"*Please*. Didn't you hear her? She's married to Jason, the guy from last night," Collette told him hatefully. "Besides, she's a surgeon. I've seen her working here before, so fat chance she'd want either of you."

"Not when she's got Jason. The two of them? Mmm, now, those would be some beautiful babies," Miranda mused before answering the phone.

"Are you friends with her?" Savannah asked, seeming as shocked as Harper felt.

"No," she answered too quickly. "I mean, I don't know. We're...neighbors."

"Two questions," James said, sliding down so that he was hanging off the back of Harper's chair. "Does she leave her bedroom windows open? And, can I move in with you?"

"Yeah, there's no way I'd let my husband look at her every day," Collette agreed. "I'd be moving."

"You guys are being ridiculous," Harper said, though her throat had gone dry. "She's just a person." She shifted in her seat, trying not to let them see that they'd spoken to her deepest fears.

"Then again, if the bedroom windows are open, I guess you'd have a pretty nice view, too, huh? Hubs is damn god-like himself," Savannah cooed.

"Oh, you think? I hadn't really noticed," Harper said stiffly, picking up the phone as soon as it began to ring.

CHAPTER EIGHT

BRYANT

Bryant smashed the last box, shoving it into the trash bins in the garage. Was it guilt that had caused him to work so hard today? Possibly. But did it matter? It wasn't like anything had really happened. So what, Tori had come over. Jason had seen Harper out and they'd talked, too. It was the same thing.

So, why had he chickened out in telling her? Was it because he knew she'd seen the evidence of what Tori had caused him to do? His towel was picked up this morning, and though he hadn't known she'd seen it for sure last night, he had his assumptions.

But, she'd never know it was Tori he was thinking about. What was more embarrassing was the wine glass. Pathetic, more like it. Touching his lips where hers had been like he was a teenager kissing a poster of Britney Spears.

If anyone ever found out, he'd be mortified. It was awful. The kind of power the woman had over him was insane. It wasn't like he'd never seen another beautiful woman. But there was something special about Tori. Sultry. Seductive. The way her eyes locked onto his, it was like she knew a secret…and hell, for all he knew she did. She could probably see the dirty thoughts racing through his mind the moment he'd laid eyes on her.

But he wasn't a cheater. He loved Harper. More than anything. He'd meant his wedding vows, and he wasn't going to end up like his parents, divorced after a lavish affair.

Not that that could happen. Women like Tori didn't want men like him.

No—shit. It wouldn't happen *because he was married.* They were both married, and that's what mattered.

He walked back through the living room and into the office, sitting down at the desk and preparing to check some emails. The school had been sending him pieces of his welcome packet, and there were a few left unopened.

He sank into the worn, leather office chair and tapped the mouse to get the screen to light up. He glanced—*it was only a glance*—out the window toward her house, and froze.

There, laying out beside the pool, was Tori. She was enclosed in the white fence that surrounded the house, but from his second story window, he had a perfect view. And what a view it was. The woman was completely topless, her brown, perfect nipples like little targets for his eyes. Her breasts were larger than he'd realized, and incredibly perky. She'd had them done, it was obvious. He'd never been much of a fake breast guy, but at the moment, it was the sexiest thing he'd ever seen.

Her tiny, blue bikini bottoms were the only thing stopping him from seeing every inch of her. She ran a hand down her thigh slowly, soaking up the sun. Her skin was porcelain, he'd never have guessed she spent much time by the pool, but she seemed quite comfortable there by the sparkling, blue water. She wore a hat, so he couldn't see her face, other than the side of her cheek and a bit of blonde hair, but somehow he knew…she wanted him to watch.

CHAPTER NINE

HARPER

Tori showed up just before four to pick her up, clad in workout gear with a blonde ponytail high on the top of her head.

"You ready to go?" she asked.

"I'm ready," Harper answered, slinging her purse over her shoulder. "I'm not sure where your gym is, but we're going to have to swing by somewhere where I can pick up a workout outfit. I'm not sure scrubs will be the best thing."

"Don't be silly," Tori told her, waving her hand as they walked out of the lobby. "I brought you an outfit."

"Oh, I don't know if yours will fit me." Tori was several inches taller, and her chest was at least a cup size larger than Harper's. Harper was sure anything that Tori had would fit awkwardly on her at best.

"Sure it will. Spandex is a godsend, after all. Come on, you can ride with me." She waved her keys in the air for emphasis and pressed a button making the blue SUV's lights flash. Harper grimaced, climbing into the car.

"So, you didn't work today?" she asked, making small talk as they pulled out of the parking lot.

Tori shook her head, her blonde hair swinging back and forth over her shoulders. "I take Thursdays as a personal day every week. It helps me focus. That way I avoid that midweek lull and come back refreshed to finish out the week. My staff can handle the minor stuff, and we schedule all of that on my day off. That way my patients get the best of me, and I'm never too drained to give them the best care."

"That's actually really smart," Harper said, thinking of the way-too-tired doctors she'd seen wandering the hospital lately. If it weren't for the also-too-tired nurses, there would be way too many errors.

"So, are you liking it here? You seem to be making some friends." She said it positively, though her words made Harper feel like a kindergartener.

"Yeah, it's all right. Still nothing like home, but I'm adjusting."

"Home…you said you're from Chicago, right?"

"Mhm," Harper said, staring out the window.

"I bet you miss it."

"Yeah, I really do."

"Do you have family there?"

"My parents and three siblings. Plus a niece."

"It must be hard…being away from them. What made you guys decide to move to Lancaster Mills? Just his job?"

"Yeah, I mean, we both applied multiple places. Obviously, my job is something I'll have to start out entry level for even though I'd like to put my degree to use soon, so it was easy enough for me to start getting offers. But, it was harder for Bryant. He didn't get many—any, really—and he'll be an excellent teacher. Really, he will. So, when Lancaster High called, we couldn't say no." She shrugged.

"You really support him," Tori said, as if it shocked her. "That's amazing of you. So many people in this world are selfish," Tori reached across the console and squeezed her hand, "but not you. That's an amazing quality, Harper."

Harper shuddered at the sound of her name. "Thank you. He'd do the same for me."

Tori let go of her hand, pulling into the parking lot of a large, tan building that looked more like a mausoleum than a gym.

"This is your gym?"

"Yep," she said, parking in a spot and climbing from the SUV. She opened the back door, grabbed a bag, and shut it again. "This is it."

"It's…strange," she said, cocking her head to the side.

"Wait 'til you see the inside." Tori took the stairs leading up to the doors two at a time with Harper trying desperately to keep up. Hell, no wonder Tori kept the body she did; getting inside her gym was a workout in and of itself.

She pulled open the door, stepping back and letting Harper enter first. When she walked in, she pulled out a badge, scanning it to go through the second set of doors. Harper reached for her wallet. "Oh, how much do I owe for coming? Or is it like a 'first time free' thing?"

Tori waved her wallet away as they entered the gym, and Harper's eyes fell to the ceiling. It was truly extraordinary with tall, expansive, ceilings allowing plenty of natural light. The gym was sectioned off into different parts. On the far right, there was a dark room with a giant screen playing *Castaway* in front of several ellipticals, bikes, and treadmills. In another section, there was a *Curves*-esque setup with several machines in a circle and women working their way around them. There was a daycare to her left, a spin class to her right, two yoga classes happening on the top floor, and further back were rooms that read 'Tanning' and 'Water Therapy.' The building was filled with every piece of workout equipment she could imagine. In short, it was beautiful. Masterfully done so that you felt comfortable right away. Employees could be seen all over, helping clients or cleaning equipment.

"This place is amazing."

"Good afternoon, Dr. Fuller," one employee greeted her.

Figures they'd know her by name.

Tori smiled at the kid before turning to Harper. "So, where would you like to go first?"

"Um, I don't know. Wherever."

"I was thinking of going for a swim," she said, pointing up above their head.

"This place has a pool?"

"Oh, sweetie, this place has everything." Without bothering to elaborate, she turned a corner, heading up a second set of stairs. *Lovely.*

Harper tried to keep up with her, though her short legs just didn't compare to the long limbs Tori had been blessed with. When they reached the second floor, Tori swiped her keycard again, pulling open a heavy gray door and holding it open again.

She smelled the chlorine before she saw it, a smell that had always taken her back to her childhood.

"Hey, guys," Tori said to a few older men who were relaxing in the shallow end. "I'm really sorry, but we're going to have to close the pool down for a few hours to get it cleaned. The filter's been giving us issues, and we want to make sure we're giving you all the best experience."

The men looked disappointed but didn't say much as they climbed out of the pool, their wet swimming suits clinging to their legs.

"When you get down there, go to the front desk and look for a man named Jamie and tell him Tori said to give you half off this month, okay? And a free smoothie from our bar."

At that, the men cheered up even more, grabbing towels

from a shelf at the end of the pool and wrapping them around their waists.

"Thank you," one of them said as the four hurried out of the room toward the sign that read 'Showers.'

Tori looked at Harper with a sly grin.

"Can you really do that?" Harper asked.

"I can do whatever I want," she sneered. *Because when you're that beautiful, you—* "I own the place."

"Y-you what?" she demanded. She knew Tori and Jason must've been well off, but this place had to be worth more money than...more money than she could even fathom. "Are you serious?"

"Dead," she said softly. "I brought you a suit." She reached in her duffel bag, pulling out a small red piece of fabric that could hardly be called a suit.

Harper examined it, trying hard not to let her face turn red from the embarrassment she felt. She was more of a one-piece girl, but how was she supposed to tell Tori that?

"You don't like it?" Tori asked, reading her expression. She walked over to the door, setting a closed sign outside of it and locking it behind her.

"No, it's fine," Harper said. "Just maybe not my—"

"'Cause you could always go naked."

Tori wasn't looking at her as she said it, though her voice echoed through the quiet pool room.

Harper looked down, completely mortified. What the hell had she gotten herself into? She let out a nervous laugh. "This is fine. Really. Where can I change?"

"Right here," Tori told her, walking back toward her and pulling out a navy bathing suit for herself. "*Come on,* we're friends, right? What? Do you need me to turn around?" She quickly peeled off the spandex workout top, letting her breasts flop out. Harper looked away quickly.

"You're super sheltered, aren't you?"

"Sheltered?" Harper asked, not looking at her but also not wanting to seem like such a kid.

"Yeah. You work at a hospital. Are you telling me you don't see naked people all day long?" She pulled the blue top over her head and Harper looked back.

"Not really, that's usually more of a nurse thing. I just see them as they're checking in."

"But you have seen naked people before, right? Besides Bryant, I mean?" She pulled down her pants, stark naked from the waist down without warning, and Harper averted her eyes without turning her head.

"Of course."

"So, what's the big deal? I'm a doctor. I literally see naked people for a living. It's natural, doll. But, if it really bothers you, there's a dressing room down that way." She pointed in the direction the men had gone before running and diving into the pool. Water splashed up onto the concrete, soaking Harper's tennis shoes.

She watched Tori swim through the water, looking completely and utterly carefree. Suddenly, a competitive nerve was struck. No way was she going to be one-upped by this girl.

She pulled her own shirt off, trying to keep her breasts somewhat hidden as sl ; pulled on the red top. When she pulled down the bottoms, she couldn't help noticing that Tori's eyes were glued to her. It was almost like it was a game. She was *trying* to see how uncomfortable she could make her. And, unfortunately, she was excellent at it.

She pulled on the bottoms, walking cautiously to the edge and sinking into the water.

"Atta girl," Tori said, running her hands over her own hair. Her stiff nipples poked through the thin material of her bathing suit. "I told you there was nothing to be nervous about."

"I'm not nervous," Harper said, perhaps a bit too harshly.

"Easy. There's nothing wrong with being a little unsure of your body." She lay back against the side of the pool, kicking her feet out through the water.

"I'm *not* unsure of my body."

"Okay, other people's bodies, then."

Harper bit her lip. "I mean, I'm not a nurse. Or a doctor. I'm not...used to it."

"No shame in that," she said simply. "Is Bryant the only guy you've been with or something?" She let out a laugh, but stopped when Harper didn't immediately shut down her theory. Instead, she felt her face growing warm, and she knew her blush must be giving her away as Tori's eyes lit up. "*Holy shit*, I was kidding. But, I'm right, aren't I?"

Harper shook her head. "I was with one other guy in college."

"Just one? Two men your entire life? *Holy shit.* No wonder you were so nervous." She scratched her head, staring at her in shock. "You've at least kissed other people, right?"

"Just the two."

"Man," Tori said, her mouth slung open in shock.

Harper put her head under water, wanting it to go quiet for just a moment, but came back up, running her hands through her own hair to match Tori. She crossed her arms. "Yep. I'm pretty shy, I guess. I hadn't really dated that much before Bryant. I'm guessing you've been with a lot of people?"

Tori frowned. "Actually, I haven't been with anyone but Jason since I was sixteen. But, before that, yeah...I was with a lot of guys."

"*Before sixteen?*" Harper couldn't hide her shock.

"Perks of being a foster brat," she said, looking away.

"I'm sorry," Harper said, feeling like she should be, even though Tori seemed to be bragging.

She shrugged. "I got my revenge." Harper furrowed her brow, waiting for her to elaborate. "I have an amazing career, more money than I could ever need, a perfect husband," she paused, looking back to Harper slowly, "great friends."

Harper smiled. "You have a great life."

"What about you? Do you have a great life?" Tori asked, her voice low.

"I, yeah, I do. I have a great husband, a beautiful home. My career is in progress. I mean, I don't have all the money I could ever want," she joked, "but—"

"Hey." Tori shocked her by pushing off the pool's wall and moving toward her quickly. "You have me. Anything you need from now on…I'm here, okay? Name it. Whatever you want…I'll take care of you." Water dripped from her lips as she spoke, and she was uncomfortably close to her. Harper tried not to move, desperately not wanting to offend Tori.

"T-thanks," she said softly, staring into the blue-green eyes behind her dark lashes. She looked down, breaking eye contact. "But, we're okay. Especially now that we're both working."

"Good," Tori said, taking a step back but not going far. "So, between us girls…settling for one man after only being with one other, Bryant must be a pretty great lay, huh?" She winked at her. Harper should've known by now that Tori had absolutely no filter, and yet everything she said managed to shock her.

"*What?*"

Tori let out a laugh. "Oh, fine, keep all the juicy details to yourself." She pushed off of the ground, letting herself rise up above the water before sinking back into it and swimming away.

Harper let out a long breath, trying hard to collect her thoughts. This woman was such a mystery. Unlike anything she'd ever experienced. Was it the age difference? The vastly different childhoods? Maybe a Southern trait? Weren't Southern women supposed to be classy little things? One thing was for sure as she watched Tori climb out of the water, her top twisted so that one breast was nearly hanging out, and make her way to the diving board...Tori was of an entirely different species than anyone Harper had ever met. She wasn't sure exactly how to feel about that.

She jumped off the diving board, her eyes locking with Harper's just seconds before she hit the water and Harper felt cold chills trail down her spine. She wrapped her arms around her chest, trying to get the feeling to go away. It was a feeling she couldn't seem to put her finger on quite yet.

Tori swam back over to her, adjusting the suit finally so she was no longer exposed. She surprised Harper by throwing her arms around her in a hug, their bodies pressed together tightly. Harper froze, processing what was happening before she hugged her back.

"I'm so glad we're friends," Tori told her. When she pulled away, she didn't go far. Their noses were just inches apart, and Harper's breathing caught in her throat. Tori's lips parted, water dripping from her eyelashes. She leaned in, her mouth moving to Harper's for a split second in a kiss that Harper hadn't expected.

"There," Tori said, when she pulled away. "Now you've got one more person to add to your roster." She winked, and with that, she was back underwater.

Fear. That was the feeling in Harper's chest. Despite everything, the playful way Tori was acting and the way she'd opened up to her. Despite the kiss that could've made even the straightest woman question her sexuality, the only thing Harper could feel in that moment was ice cold fear.

CHAPTER TEN

BRYANT

When Harper walked in, her hair was pulled back into a wet ponytail. He closed his laptop and stared up at her.

"Whoa, some workout, huh?"

She furrowed her brow, then seemed to realize what he meant, touching her hair and shaking her head. "We went swimming."

"We?" he asked. "Who'd you go with?"

"Oh." She waved him off, hurrying past him. "Just…Tori from next door." She explained it as if Bryant wouldn't know who she meant.

He followed her down the hall and into the bedroom where she peeled off her clothes and changed into her pajamas from the bed.

"You didn't bring a suit."

"She let me borrow one."

Just like that, he was thinking of Tori in a suit. Tori splashing in the water with her long, long legs…Tori topless beside her pool.

"Why would you go to a gym to swim when she has a pool?"

Harper stopped, turning to look at him. "How do you know she has a pool?"

Panic overtook him as he tried to think quickly. "Oh, um, well, I...I saw it when we were at their house. It's in the back-yard." Harper seemed to believe him, though from the side yard where the patio was, there was little chance he could've seen the pool. She ran a brush through her long, brown hair, wringing excess water into her scrubs and tossing them into the hamper. "Anyway, why'd you go workout with her? I thought you didn't like her."

"I'm trying to be civil," she said simply, not meeting his eye. "She's our neighbor, right? Nothing about that is chang-ing, so we might as well all get along."

He nodded. "Yeah, you're right." And she was. As much as it pained him to think about Harper and Tori hanging out, as if Tori might somehow know the effect she had on him and use Harper to toy with him, there was nothing he could do, no reason he could give his wife to make her see why this could be an issue. *No reason that wouldn't end with a swift kick in the balls, anyway.* He was terrified of being in the same room with the two of them, fearful that Harper would sense the awkward energy between Tori and himself—especially after their last encounter, but there was nothing that could be done.

"Hey," she said, suddenly spinning around on the stool in front of her vanity. For a half-second as their eyes met, he panicked, worrying that she knew what he was thinking. "I need to tell you something."

He sat down on the edge of the bed, leaning over his knees and staring back at her, his throat suddenly dry. "Okay."

"Something happened today. It was...stupid. You're going

to laugh." By the look in her eyes, he was fairly certain he wasn't going to be laughing. "But," she tucked a piece of hair behind her ears, looking down, "I don't know, I just feel like I need to tell you."

He reached for her hands. "What is it, babe? You're scaring me."

"I, um, well…Tori kind of…she *kissed* me."

No matter what he had thought she was going to say—every variation of horrible things—nothing would've ever prompted him to predict that sentence leaving her mouth. His brain wasn't computing her words. He sat still, staring at her with his mouth hung open, picturing it over and over. Tori's lips on Harper's. Hands exploring. Tongues tangled.

He closed his eyes, running a palm over his face. "Um, what?"

"I mean, it wasn't, you know, like a *kiss* kiss. It was…just goofing off, I guess. I don't really know what to call it. She was teasing me about having only been with you and Trevor. It wasn't a big deal, so I don't know why I'm making it a big deal, but I wanted to tell you about it. I don't know if it's cheating. I didn't want to kiss her. I love you so much, and I—"

"Baby—" He cut her off, pulling her to him. She stood from the stool, sulking her way to him slowly. "I'm not mad at you."

"You're not?" Her eyes lit up at his words, and he realized she'd truly been worried about it.

"Not at all. I mean," he laughed, "it's a little weird, but also kind of hot."

She raised an eyebrow. "Oh, it is, is it?"

"Yeah," he whispered, nuzzling into her neck.

"Well, don't get any ideas. It's never going to happen again."

He sucked in a deep breath, sliding his hands under her

shirt to remove it. "For the next fifteen minutes, let's just pretend it might."

CHAPTER ELEVEN

BRYANT

"No, it went really well," Bryant told his wife over the phone. It was his first day of work. With the school year just beginning, he was already feeling sluggish and worn down after a day of giving lectures to bratty teenagers. But, telling Harper any of that would do nothing to help him. She was stuck at work for the next several hours, and having her feeling bad for him would only make him feel worse. So, he lied. Like he'd gotten so good at doing lately.

"I'm glad, baby. I'm so proud of you. My sexy little teacher," she said with a giggle, and he could hear her voice lower as she said the word *sexy*.

"I miss you," he said softly. "I really wish you were off early tonight. I need a drink."

"I know," she whispered. "Maybe I could pretend I've come down with something. Collette went home with a stomach virus earlier this week."

"No," he said with a sigh. "It's okay. I don't want you to get in trouble. I'm just gonna head home and collapse anyway. I'm exhausted."

"Well, I made some spaghetti for dinner. You can just heat it up and relax."

"Thanks, babe. How's your day going so far?"

"Fine," she said stiffly. "Speaking of…I'm going to have to go. I'm pulling into work now."

"Okay. I love you," he said, hearing her car shut off through the phone.

"I love you, too," she said. "Be careful going home."

"Have a good night." He pulled the phone away from his ear, pressing the red button that would end the call. A knock on his window caused him to jerk forward, and he looked up, shocked to see Tori standing just beyond the glass. She wore a floor-length black gown and a large, white hat as if she were going to attend a derby soon. It was all very extravagant for an afternoon at the high school. He rolled down his window. "Tori?"

"Hey," she said casually, resting her arm on the window of his car. "Rough day, stud?"

He recalled the story of her and Harper in the pool almost instantly. Should he tell her he knew? Would she bring it up? He shook his head. "Not too bad."

"You're a better man than I am. These kids are animals." As if on cue, a group of teenage boys strolled past, one of them letting out a wolf-whistle as the others laughed and cheered him on. Tori hardly budged, rolling her eyes at them, but not looking away from Bryant.

"Yeah, you could say that again. What are you so dressed up for?"

"This old thing?" She waved a hand dismissively, a smirk on her face. "Nah, I was supposed to go to this gala tonight. I partner up with the school every year, do some charity surgery. But, apparently it got canceled, and the secretary here *forgot that email was a thing*," she said through gritted teeth.

"A gala?" he asked. "Well, that's fancy."

"When you've seen one, you've seen them all." She bobbed her head up. "Where are you headed?"

"Home," he said, resting his hand on the wheel. He surprised himself by feeling less nervous around her than before. Perhaps he was growing used to her overwhelming beauty. It was like being in the presence of a celebrity, but he guessed even celebrities got boring after a while.

"Home? *What?* No way. Call Harper. I'll see what Jay is doing…let's all go out for a drink and celebrate."

"Celebrate?"

"Today was your first day of work, right?"

"I don't know if that's really a reason to celebrate."

She leaned down further in the window, and suddenly he could smell her perfume. It smelled of cinnamon. "Every day has a reason to celebrate if you look hard enough." She pulled out her cell phone. "Oh, come on. You look like you could use a drink."

He nodded, unable to deny that. "Yeah, but Harper's stuck at work. She's on seconds this week."

"Ah," she said, staring at her phone screen. "Jay's got a deadline for one of his articles, too." She pressed her lips into a fine line, staring at her phone in dismay. After a minute, she slid it back into her white, leather purse. "Oh, well, more for us, right?" She patted his arm. "What do you say? Let me buy you a drink?"

"Uh, I don't know if that's such a good idea."

"Why not?" she challenged. "We're all friends here, right?"

He swallowed, thinking of just how good of *friends* she and Harper were. "Well, yeah, but…"

"But, nothing. Come on, I'm paying. You drive." She walked around to the passenger's side and climbed in without waiting for permission. She looked up at him as she buckled her seatbelt, leaning over so that he had a view straight down her dress for just a second. She looked up, catching him staring seconds before he looked away, but she didn't say anything.

"Are you sure Jason's going to be okay with this?" he asked, his hands off the wheel as if that might stop what was happening.

She took her hat off, flipping down the mirror to check her hair. "Does he have a reason not to be?" she asked him, her eyes meeting his in the reflection.

"No, of course not."

"Then, drive," she said, closing the mirror and giving him a wink. "And don't even think about going slow."

"Huh?" he asked, a breath catching in his chest.

"You heard me," she told him, sticking her hand out the window. "I've been dying to ride you since I saw you move in."

He swallowed, and then again, hard. "Excuse me?"

She turned to look at him finally, an innocent look in her eyes. "I said I've been dying to ride with you since I saw you move in. Jason never liked sports cars. He's all about statistics and facts...and, well, they aren't the safest. Me, I like a little danger." She let the word hang on her tongue, their eyes locked together. "All in the name of good fun, right?" She batted her eyelashes at him.

"Yeah," he whispered, unable to pull his gaze from her. He couldn't believe she'd called his car a *sports car,* though he guessed it technically was. His reliable old Pontiac Solstice had once been a thing of beauty, long before he'd gotten it in high school, but it was up there in years, and there was nothing spectacular about it anymore. After what seemed like an eternity, she looked back out the window.

"Well, what are you waiting on, Bryant? Are we doing this thing or what?"

It was a game. A challenge. One he should've said no to. One he should've asked her to stop playing. Instead, he found himself turning the key in the ignition, wanting to see exactly what they were playing for.

CHAPTER TWELVE

BRYANT

W hen they arrived at the restaurant, Bryant's nerves had all but disappeared. Tori had been normal the rest of the way. She'd joked with him about work, swapping spouse stories, complaining about the heat. It was almost as if they truly could be friends.

As long as he didn't look at her.

As long as she didn't touch him. At all.

He held the door open for her as she walked through, and refused to let his eyes go further than her shoulders. Being good was the only option. *Behaving.* Sure, he knew he should've texted Harper to let her know what was up, but what would she say? He hadn't gotten mad when she'd hung out with Jason, after all. But was that different? They hadn't actively gone out together. *As far as he knew, anyway.* Who was he kidding? He knew what he was doing was wrong. The guilty lump sat in the pit of his stomach.

As he mused about it, he lost control of his eyes, and they somehow ended up on Tori's ass, watching it sway as she made her way across the floor. She sank into a booth before a waiter could seat them, obviously familiar with this place.

He picked up a menu from the table, searching for something to eat, but she pulled it from his hands as a waiter came by. "Two scotches. On the rocks with a twist." She handed the menus back, folding her hands in front of her.

He cleared his throat. "No food?"

"I'm sorry, were you hungry?" She cocked her head to the side. "I just assumed you were waiting for Harper to get home to eat."

He lowered his brow. "Yeah, good point. So, scotch, huh?"

"Shoot. I'm doing it again, aren't I? I have this tendency to…take control. Jason hates it. Do you want me to order you something else? It's a bad habit, I know."

"No," he said, reaching up to adjust the blind so the light wouldn't burn his eyes. "It's fine. Scotch works."

"It's a celebration," she said happily, taking the drinks as they appeared moments later.

He clinked his glass against hers, taking a sip and feeling the unfamiliar burn. He was mostly a beer guy. Hard liquor had never really been his thing, but his ego wasn't going to let him turn away the drink as Tori downed hers in front of him and ordered another before the waiter had gotten too far out of sight.

"Wow. Well, you just put me to shame."

She laughed. "I'm a doctor, Bry. We drink and we over-charge people for unnecessary medical care." She shrugged her shoulders. "It's what we do."

Bry. He hung on her every word, loving the sound of the pet name coming out of her mouth. No one had ever given him a nickname before. Bryant was already short enough. But, somehow this worked.

He took another drink, the heat filling his body already. It was strong, and on an empty stomach, it would work fast. He needed to pace himself. He set the drink down.

"So, did Harper tell you what happened at the gym?" she asked, staring up at him from behind her dark lashes.

He flushed even warmer. "Um...what do you mean?"

"Please," she said, kicking her leg out so it hit him under the table. To his surprise, once their legs connected, she didn't move hers away. "I know she did, or you wouldn't be that red. Your eyes are doing that 'deer in the headlights' thing."

He laughed, looking down and running his hand through his hair. "Yeah, she may have mentioned it."

"Are you mad at me?" she teased.

"No," he said simply, not sure what else to say.

"Good," she said, running her leg over his again and pushing his drink further toward him, urging him to indulge more. She held up her glass. "I really want us to all be friends."

He picked his up slowly, touching it to hers as she waited for him to drink before she did. "We are friends," he told her as she licked a bit of her drink off her top lip.

She nodded. "Awesome. Oh, and I'm sorry about the other day."

"The other day?" he asked.

"You know...when you saw me out by the pool." Her leg was still on his; there was no way she couldn't tell it was him and not the table leg that she was rubbing against. "That house has been empty for a long time. I'm used to being able to...lay out without worrying who sees."

He sucked down a bit of his drink, inhaling sharply and coughing as he realized what she was talking about. "Shit, Tori, I'm sorry," he said through his coughs, feeling utterly humiliated.

"No, don't be. I'm the one who should be apologizing. I'll try to be more careful next time."

He nodded, swirling his drink and wishing like hell he

could've gone back in time and left the school's parking lot a few minutes sooner. Actually, if he was making wishes, he'd rather wish he could go back to that day and never have been watching in the first place.

"Hey, listen, you didn't mention that to Harper, did you?" he asked, his voice low.

She looked serious, her lips parted slightly, and when she spoke, it was a vow. "No. Never, Bryant. I would never tell her. It's our little secret."

CHAPTER THIRTEEN

BRYANT

Bryant stopped after two drinks, but judging from the way his skin was buzzing as he dropped her back at her house, he should've stopped sooner. She sat in the passenger's seat, unmoving. In fact, she hadn't spoken in so long, he was sure she was asleep.

He put the car in park at the end of her driveway, looking over at her. "Well, thanks for the drinks."

She smiled at him in the dark car, only the dash lights illuminating her perfect face. "You're welcome."

He cleared his throat. "Well, I'd better get home."

She nodded. "I had a lot of fun tonight."

"Yeah, me too. We'll have to do it again."

She seemed to like that idea, her arms suddenly reaching out as she leaned in to give him a hug. "Are you sure you're okay leaving your car at the school?" he asked. "I can drive Jason up there if he needs to go get it."

She shook her head, her face still nuzzled into his neck. "I'll have him take me to the school in the morning to pick it up." Her lips grazed his skin, and she pulled away slowly. The entire thing seemed to happen in slow motion. Her eyes met his, their noses touching, and his gaze fell to her lips. He started to open his mouth, to tell her all the reasons why this couldn't happen, but their mouths were on each other's, on fire, in an instant. She tasted of scotch and cinnamon gum, her plump lips like little treats for him to devour. She wrapped her hands around his neck, her fingers tugging at his hair. Their mouths explored fervently; he couldn't taste her quickly enough.

He licked her neck, his tongue trailing across her skin slowly, sensually. Her moan was electrifying, his body responding instantly. He moved his hands to her breasts, his palm partially on the dress that prevented full access, and partially on her skin. He wanted underneath the dress, inside of her. She seemed to understand, climbing over onto his lap instantly. They were teenagers—wild and animal-like as they groped each other in the car, just praying not to get caught. She pulled her dress off her shoulders, allowing her breasts to fall free, and he scooped them up, running his tongue across the nipples he'd only been able to admire from afar. She pulled her dress up around her waist, sticking her fingers between her legs to pull her panties to the side as he worked to free his erection.

She put her hands onto the ceiling as he slid into her, his entire body shaking from contact with her skin, with her most private parts. It was intense. He'd never known sex like this. Sex that could light you on fire with just a touch. He lifted her up, letting her skin bounce off of his slowly, trying to hold off the orgasm he could already feel brimming.

He wanted to please her. He wanted her to finish first. To remember this time with him as an experience that changed her. He wanted her to feel the earth shatter as he pulsed inside of her, but as she looked down, her breasts bouncing and her smoldering eyes begging him for more, he knew he didn't stand much chance.

She leaned down, her lips on his ear. "Please don't stop, Bryant," she begged, her tongue teasing his ear lobe. She bit down. "Don't stop until you've put a baby in me."

He froze.

He hadn't worn a condom.

This had to stop before—

She pulsed up and down again, giving him one last second before he felt his body release, sending him over the edge.

Fuck.

CHAPTER FOURTEEN

BRYANT

Bryant showered that night, trying to beat the clock before Harper made it home. He couldn't believe what he'd done. Already, the stress and guilt of his actions were weighing on him. How could he have been so stupid? How would he ever keep this from Harper? Would Tori tell Jason? They hadn't talked about it after; he merely pulled up his pants as she adjusted her dress and they walked away, neither even saying goodbye. What they'd done was unspeakable, and so they did not speak. Not of this night. Not ever again.

But what if he'd actually gotten her pregnant? He pressed his fists into his face, praying he hadn't. It would destroy his life. It would destroy his marriage. Tori wasn't who he wanted. Sure, she was gorgeous. But she wasn't Harper. She couldn't make him laugh on cue like his wife could. She didn't know that he preferred vegetable over chicken noodle soup when he was sick. She didn't know that he'd choose pizza over steak any night of the week. She wasn't his wife. And he'd made a terrible, terrible mistake.

He let out a loud sob, sinking to his knees. In his weakest moment, he'd become his father—the one man he'd sworn to never be. No, he was worse. Not even a year into their marriage, and he'd done what it had taken his father seven years to do, or at least confess to.

How would he ever survive this? Harper wouldn't forgive him. She couldn't. And could he blame her? Of course not. The worst part was that, even if they could somehow move past this, they'd have Tori next door to them forever. Everyday—this living, breathing reminder of what he'd done.

"Bryant?" the voice startled him, and he shot up from his knees, slipping on the slick floor—*she'd told him they needed a bath mat*—and slamming down onto his back. "Oh, god," she cried, rushing to him and opening the curtain quickly to stare at her broken husband.

He lay on the floor, tears mixed with water on his face so she couldn't tell the difference. His back burned from slamming onto the acrylic siding of the tub, but as far as he could tell, nothing was badly hurt. "Babe?"

"Are you okay?" she asked, holding out a hand to help him up.

"Yeah," he said, heaving a breath as he stood slowly. "You're home early."

"I am. I talked the guys into covering for me so I could get an extra hour with you. Why are you showering so late? Did I hear you crying?" She cocked her head to the side, one arm drenched from the water. He shut the faucet off and grabbed a towel from the wall, running it over his face and chest while trying to decide what the hell he was going to tell her.

Without too much thought, he realized what he had to do. What he'd always known he was going to do. "I came home and crashed," he explained. "Then I woke up and wanted to get a shower before tomorrow. I was trying to get done before you got home so we could spend some time together."

"So, you weren't crying?" she asked.

"No," he said. "Yawning, maybe?" He faked a yawn. "I'm still half asleep, I think. Explains why I forgot how to stand up."

She stared at him, and he wondered if she could read the lie all over his face, but she finally shrugged. "Mind if I join you?"

He nodded, turning the water back on and stepping out of the stream as she peeled off her clothes, stepping into the water. "I've missed you," she whispered, pulling him down into a kiss. He pulled away, probably too sharply. "Ahh, I see why you fell asleep. Is that alcohol I taste?" she teased.

"Yeah," he said, laughing nervously and wondering what else she could taste. God, he was such an asshole. "You caught me."

CHAPTER FIFTEEN

HARPER

When Harper got home from work a few nights later, she walked into a dark living room, jumping at the sight waiting for her as she flipped on the light. Bryant lay on the couch, his cheek bloody and swollen and his bottom lip busted.

"Oh my god!" she cried, dropping her purse and rushing toward him.

He shot up, looking dazed as he tried to adjust to his surroundings. "What's wrong?" he asked.

"*What's wrong?* What happened to you?" she demanded.

He winced, touching a finger to his lip. "Ouch. Sorry, I didn't mean to scare you. I'm fine."

"You don't look fine," she argued. "What happened?"

He stood, walking past her and into the kitchen quickly, his tone defensive. "I'm fine, honestly."

"Why won't you tell me what happened? You're all beaten up, Bryant. You look like you've been in a fight."

He sighed, grabbing a beer from the fridge and turning back around to face her with a look of shame. "I was...mugged."

She hurried toward him again, but he wouldn't let her touch his face. "Mugged? What do you mean, mugged?"

"What do you think I mean? I was mugged, okay? No big deal. I'm fine, like I said."

"How did it happen? When did it happen? What did they take?" she demanded, her voice growing loud with worry. She searched him for more signs of harm, lifting his arms up as he pulled them away from her.

"After school. I walked down the street to grab some more beer from the liquor store. I shouldn't have gone down the alley. It was stupid."

"And someone attacked you?"

He scowled, taking a drink with an angry groan. "I mean, it isn't like they punched me. I could've taken them if they'd come at me from the front. They shoved me down from behind. I wouldn't have even fallen if I wasn't completely caught off guard. My cheek hit the pavement, that's it. Probably just a bunch of stupid kids looking to get one over on their teacher."

"Did you call the police?"

He pursed his lips. "No, there'd be no use. They only grabbed the spare cash I had in my hand from where I'd just paid, plus the beer and my keys. I should've stuck the cash into my pocket right away, but…I mean, it's a small town. We aren't in Chicago anymore. I'm more mad about the beer than anything," he said with a playful laugh.

"They took your keys?"

His eyes rolled back in frustration. "Yeah. I mean, it's a pain, but I'm just glad it wasn't my wallet. Thank God your dad got us that hide-a-key magnet thing to put under the car, or I'd've had to call you to come pick me up. We'll have to get some new ones made this weekend. All in all, not the worst thing that could've happened. I'm not even that sore. Just wish I could've caught the dumbasses who did it. Wouldn't that have been something?"

"I'm so sorry, Bryant," she said, brushing a finger over his wound. He didn't seem to want her to fuss over him, but he didn't resist.

"I'll be fine, babe. Don't make a big deal out of it."

"Are you sure you're okay? Did you put ice on it so it doesn't bruise?"

"Yes," he said, placing the bottle of beer on his wound as proof.

"I hate that that happened. You're right, though. Lancaster Mills seems so quaint, I can't believe something like that could happen here. Maybe we ought to call the police just to be on the safe side."

"And tell them what? Someone stole twelve dollars from me?"

"And your keys! They could get into our home, take our cars. The police should know that."

"They won't know whose house or car those keys go to."

"But if it was one of your students—"

"Go ahead and call them if you want," he said finally. "But I'm telling you it's silly. My students aren't going to go to prison over stealing my Pontiac, I can guarantee you that."

She let out a breath, trying not to laugh at the thought. She wasn't sure how he could be so cavalier about everything. "You still should've called me."

"For what? I'm fine, Harp." He kissed her forehead. "It looks worse than it feels, and aside from the fact that this is my last beer, there was no real harm done." He downed the last of his drink on cue and tossed it into the trash. "Now, you look exhausted. What do you say we get to bed?"

CHAPTER SIXTEEN

HARPER

The next weekend, Bryant woke up early and headed out, claiming he was going to get new keys made. He'd hinted that he also had something he wanted to surprise her with, but she couldn't imagine what. Harper took the opportunity to take a long bath and get started cleaning the kitchen.

Growing up, her mother had dedicated Saturday mornings to cleaning house, and it was something she actually grew to enjoy as a kid. They'd turn the music up loud, each person picking a room and cleaning. With two sisters and an older brother, plus her parents, the house was usually cleaned within an hour, and then they had the rest of the day to spend relaxing.

Just thinking about those mornings made her homesick. She missed her family. She missed her friends. But more than anything, she missed having a house full of people. Lately, it was just her and Bryant, and it was starting to get lonely with their conflicting schedules.

She couldn't put into words how grateful she was to finally have a weekend off, the first one since they'd moved to Lancaster Mills. She glanced at the clock. Bryant had been gone just over an hour. Where could he be? She ran the towel over the final dish, stacking it into the cabinet and turning around to lean on the counter, letting out a breath.

Her phone chimed across the room, and she hurried over to it, wondering who it could be and hoping it was him. Instead, it was a meme from Savannah making fun of their boss. She responded back with three laughing emojis for effect and set the phone down. Then, she picked it back up. Seriously. Where the hell could he be?

Just then, the doorbell rang and she began to imagine the worst. With shaking hands, her phone in one squeezed palm, she walked to the door. In Chicago, you didn't answer the door. People called first, or they weren't people you wanted to see. But, apparently it was different here.

She pulled open the door, shocked to see Jason standing there. "Jason," she said, feeling self conscious about her suds-covered shirt and ratty ponytail. "Is everything okay?"

He smiled at her, his grin wide and friendly. "Yeah, of course. Did I catch you at a bad time?" he asked.

"No, sorry. I was just cleaning." She stepped back, holding an arm out to let him come in.

He stepped into her home, wiping his shoes on the mat respectfully before stepping onto the carpet. "Is Bryant home?"

"Oh, no. He just stepped out. He should be home any minute, though."

"Damn," he said, shaking his head.

"What's up?"

"Nothing. I needed some help with the garden. I was gonna see if he wanted to get his hands dirty."

"The garden?" she said with a teasing sneer. "Don't you have people who do that for you?"

He smiled. "Actually, it kind of relaxes me."

She sighed. "Kind of like cleaning for me, I guess."

He nodded slowly before letting a small smile spread across his lips. "Now *that* I hire out for."

"You know, I guess I could help you."

"Really?" he asked, seeming shocked.

"Yeah, I used to help my dad with the garden every summer. What are you planting?"

"Just flowers," he said. "Tori likes fresh flowers every fall, so I usually get them started in August. You don't have to help, though. Honestly, I just—"

"I don't mind. Really, I don't. It would be nice to feel a bit more at home here. Bryant can help, too, when he gets back. I think he'd like that."

"Yeah?"

"Yeah," she said happily. "Let me run and change real quick."

"Okay," he said, rubbing the back of his arm over his forehead. "Dress cool, though. It's a scorcher out there."

She nodded, hurrying to her room to change and sending Bryant a quick text to let him know where she'd be when he came home. She didn't wait for his response, laying her phone down and rushing out after Jason, trying to assure herself her excitement could only stem from doing something that made her feel close to her parents. It had absolutely nothing to do with the beautiful specimen she'd be working alongside.

"You ready?" he asked, holding the door open for her as she walked out. She turned to lock her doors. "You don't have to do that," he said with a laugh. "You'll just be right over there."

She slid the key into her pocket, smiling at him sheepishly. "Force of habit."

"So, how are you liking life here in Lancaster Mills?" he

asked, shielding his eyes from the sun as he spoke. "I imagine it's pretty different than what you were used to."

"It is for sure," she said. "But...it's nice. Just in different ways."

He nodded, stopping in his front yard and grabbing the wheelbarrow filled with bags of soil. "We're working around here." He nodded his head toward the back yard, and she raced ahead, swinging the fence open to let him in.

"What about you?" she asked as he set the soil down, tearing it open and pouring a bag into the empty flower bed that sat near their patio. "Tori mentioned you guys were from Tennessee. Anywhere near a city? Nashville? Memphis?"

He shook his head. "Nah, Asheville was the closest city, and that was still a good hour. We've always lived in the country."

"Wow. It's crazy. I never would've pictured that. You guys don't come across 'small town' at all." She cringed. "I hope that didn't come out wrong. I don't mean it bad, honestly. I guess I just always had this picture of how small-town people lived and acted, and well...you just weren't what I expected."

He tipped an imaginary cowboy hat, pretending to take a toothpick from his mouth and grinned. "Well, thank ya, ma'am."

She laughed. "I know. I shouldn't make assumptions."

"It's okay," he told her. "When the realtor told us people from Chicago were moving in, we assumed you guys would be assholes, so I guess we're even." He picked up another bag, a smirk on his face as he laid it down.

"Thanks a lot."

"I said we *thought*. Luckily, you both proved us wrong." He paused, wiping his forehead. "Hey, I'll be right back. You can go ahead and start emptying this bag if you want." He darted in the house as she tore open the bag.

She was halfway through the next one when he returned, several minutes later, carrying two glasses of iced tea.

"Took you long enough," she joked. "I thought you were going to make me do all the work."

"Nah, just most of it." He set the drinks next to her and bent down, beginning to help her level the soil. She stayed on her knees next to him, the paved stones of the patio digging into her bare knees and causing her to wish she'd worn something other than shorts.

"Thanks for this," she told him, taking a sip of the too-sweet tea. She tried not to make a face.

"I guess I didn't do so well," he said, not missing her sour expression. "I tried to put less sugar than usual for you. Blame it on my Southerness." He looked over at her, their brown eyes connecting.

"Thank you. That was sweet of you." After a moment, she looked down, tucking a piece of loose hair out of sight and reaching into the soil to help him smooth it out. "So, where's Tori today? Is she going to be helping?"

He shook his head. "She had to go to town earlier. She'll be back this afternoon, but...gardening isn't really her thing."

Harper wondered if Tori had told her husband what happened to them in the pool. Feeling mortified, she forced herself to think of something, anything, else. "What is her thing?" she asked. "I mean, what does she like to do? Besides fix people's faces."

He let out a loud laugh. "What does my wife like to do? That's a good question." He scratched his chin with his shoulder, grabbing a few plants and divvying them out between himself and Harper. "She...she likes wine and trashy TV. She likes to shop. She likes to sit in coffee shops and people watch. Oh," he pointed to the pool behind them, "and she likes to swim." He winked at her, and in that moment, she knew he knew.

"Oh."

He shook his head. "Truth is, she's still a mystery to me, even to this day. I feel like I've known her my whole life, and I still learn new things about her all the time."

"That's what keeps things exciting, right? I mean, I *hope* I don't know everything about Bryant."

His eyebrows shot up and he frowned, but he looked away quickly enough for her to question what she'd seen. "I'm sure you don't."

"What's that mean?" she asked, sensing his ominous tone. He continued to work, not speaking for a moment. Finally, as he patted the soil down around the flower in front of him, pressing it carefully into place and reaching over to help her with hers, he sighed.

"Just that you can never truly know someone. Not as much as you'd think."

CHAPTER SEVENTEEN

BRYANT

B ryant got the text message from Harper while Tori was laying face down on her desk in front of him. The woman was like his kryptonite. He was hypnotized around her. Powerless. The text message seemed to break the spell. He froze, stepping back and letting go of her waist as he stared down at the phone in his free hand.

"Shit," he said, pulling up his pants.

"What?" she asked. "What is it?"

"Harper is with Jason."

"So?" She pulled her skirt down, obviously not worried about the potential crisis he was sure would occur if their spouses got together.

"*So?* So, what happens when they realize we're both gone? We have to get back." She took the phone from his hand, and he grabbed it back quickly, anger welling in his chest.

"Then what happens when they realize we're both coming back at the same time? Come on, Jason thinks I'm at work…which isn't technically a lie," she pointed around her office, "and you're supposed to be at the store. They won't suspect anything."

He closed his eyes, stepping back from her as she moved forward. "I can't do this right now, Tori. I came here to tell you we can't do this anymore. That's why I was here. I can't be with you anymore."

"Well, you sure as hell didn't have a problem the last time. Or five minutes ago, for that matter."

"I'm feeling guilty. I love my wife. I…I don't know what comes over me when I'm around you. That's why I've stayed away. When you asked me to meet you today, I was relieved. I've wanted to talk to you—"

"I've wanted to talk to you, too," she said, reaching for him.

He pushed her hand away. "Not like that. This can't happen. *This*. Whatever this is. Us. It's over. We're over. I don't want to see you again. Not as friends, not as anything."

"You can't be serious," she sneered. "You really think you can walk away from me so easily?"

"Yeah, I can. This was a mistake…all of it. I should have never done this. I should've never come here." He turned around, rushing out of her office.

Her heels clicked as they hurried along the linoleum. "Bryant, wait!" she called, but he ignored her. "*Wait!*" she screamed, grabbing for his back, suddenly closer than he'd realized.

He spun around. "Stay away from me, Tori. I mean it. Don't come near me or Harper ever again."

"Or what?" she asked, rearing back her head, looking utterly mortified. It was obvious she wasn't used to being told 'no.'

He furrowed his brow, opening his car door. "Just…just don't, okay?" He pointed his keys at her. "I mean it."

She crossed her arms over her chest, looking furious as he drove away. She wasn't happy, but she'd get over it. She had to. They both did. This wasn't anything that could last. He'd sooner die than break Harper's heart. He just wished he'd realized that before...*this*.

CHAPTER EIGHTEEN

HARPER

"There," Jason said, standing back from their work and dusting off his knees. "You do good work, Page."

She smiled. "So do you...hey, how do you know our last name?" she asked, staring at him strangely.

He smirked. "Um, it's on your mailbox?" He stared back at her, and she realized he was right, though she'd never thought to check for theirs. "I pay attention to things," he said softly, and the way he said it gave her chills.

"What kind of things?" she asked, wrapping her hand around her elbow.

"Just...everything. I'm a writer, after all. It's kind of my job to notice things other people don't."

"And my last name is one of those things?"

He nodded. "Do you know mine?"

It was as if he'd read her mind. She glanced at the ground, staring back up with one eye closed and a furrowed brow from the bright sun, trying desperately to remember because she was almost certain she had heard it before. "I never checked."

He laughed. "See, things people don't notice."

She nodded, wiping off her knees again. She was completely covered in dirt. "It's Fuller, by the way," he told her. "My—*our*—last name."

"Well, nice to officially meet you, Jason Fuller," she replied, suddenly remembering hearing it at the gym the other day.

"I'm going to go grab a drink. Do you want one?" he offered.

"Oh, no, I really think I should get home. I need a shower, and Bryant should be home any minute."

"You could always go for a swim instead," he told her, making her face warm again. What was it with these people and swimming?

"No, really, that's okay. He'll be waiting for me."

"Are you sure about that?" he asked, stepping closer toward her.

She looked down and then back up again. "What do you mean? Why wouldn't he be?"

He reached out, touching her arm where her dirty handprint was. "It's just…it's like I said, I notice things."

"Meaning what, Jason? What have you noticed?" Her heart was pounding in her chest. He knew something. She could see it in his eyes. But what was it? What did he know? He looked down as if he didn't want to tell her, but she stepped even closer. "Tell me," she dared him.

They were dangerously close now, their torsos practically touching as she begged him to speak. When he looked up, his eyes held a sorrow she hadn't been expecting. "I just—"

"Harper?" She spun around, staring at Bryant. He stood behind the white gate, a stunned look on his face. "What's going on?"

She practically jumped away from Jason, looking guilty as sin. "Hey," she squeaked. "Did you get my text?"

He nodded, his eyes squaring with Jason's as he walked through the gate. "What's going on?" he repeated.

Harper stepped in front of him. "We were doing some gardening. I was hoping you'd get back in time to help." She patted his chest. "Where were you, anyway? You've been gone for, like, three hours."

He shook his head. "I told you I had to run to town."

"You guys are welcome to stay for lunch, if you'd like," Jason said politely. "I'm assuming Tori will be back anytime *also*."

Something in his words caused Harper's stomach to lurch, but before she could dwell on it, Bryant grabbed her hand, lacing his fingers through hers. "No, we should get home." It was obviously not up for discussion at that point. "Come on, Harper."

"Thank you for all of your help, Harper," Jason called after them. "I'll see you around."

She waved a hand in his direction, though she wasn't completely listening, because Tori's SUV was pulling into the garage at that exact moment, and Jason's words were echoing in her head: *I notice things.*

CHAPTER NINETEEN

HARPER

When they got back to the house, Bryant released her hand almost instantly.

"I'm going to take a shower," she said, slipping off her shoes and laying them on the mat.

"What were you doing with him?" he demanded, swirling around to face her with a heated rage.

"Excuse me?" she asked. "What do you mean what was I doing with him?"

"Why were you over there, Harper? Why were you over there *alone* with the man next door?"

She scoffed. "Uh, probably because he came over to ask you for help, and you weren't here—God only knows why—and so I offered. Where were *you,* anyway?"

"Don't turn this around on me," he said hatefully.

"No, I *am* turning it around on you," she said, as the thought occurred to her. "You were supposed to be going out to get me a surprise. So, where is it?" She held out her hand.

He clenched his fists to his sides. "You don't get to just change the subject like this. I want to know why you were there."

"I told you why I was there. He needed help with his garden."

"Yeah, I'll bet he did." He scoffed, looking away.

"What is *that* supposed to mean?" she fumed, her whole body shaking with anger. How dare he accuse her of doing anything. How dare he assume she was with him for any reason other than the one she'd provided. He was wrong. She'd done what she said. She'd helped a neighbor. Someone he should've been here to help.

"It's supposed to mean that I don't trust him."

"You don't have to trust him, Bryant. What matters is that you trust me." She froze, trying to read his angry expression. "You *do* trust me, don't you?"

He frowned. "I don't know what to believe anymore, Harper. You're running around all the time, I come home to find you gone, you're kissing women in a gym pool."

She felt cool tears stinging her eyes. "That's what this is about? Me and Tori? Bryant, I told you about that. I told you about that as soon as it happened. You said it wasn't a big deal. You know I'm not interested in women. Tori is…I don't know what she is. A friend, maybe? But I haven't spoken to her since. You have nothing to worry about. Certainly not with her."

"And what about him? Huh? What about Jason?"

"What *about* Jason?" She shook her head, wiping away the tears from her cheeks. "Do you honestly believe I would cheat on you? I love you, Bryant. I married you. I meant what I said at that church. I would never," she took a step toward him, begging him to look her way, "*never* do anything to hurt you."

He finally looked up at her, his eyes losing themselves in hers. "I just never want to lose you."

"You won't," she promised, touching his chest.

"I want you to stay away from him. From both of them."

"They haven't done anything wrong," she argued. "They're nice people." Honestly, she wasn't sure why she was fighting so hard to keep the Fullers in her life. It wasn't like she really considered them friends, but it was nice to have neighbors you could turn to if you really needed it. Besides, Jason seemed to have information she may need, and being ordered not to see him would make learning said information much more difficult.

"I just don't trust them," he said. "We can be cordial, but I think they're trouble. Look at what they're already doing to us."

"They haven't done anything, Bryant. What's going on with you? Where have you really been today?"

He closed his eyes, pinching the bridge of his nose between his thumb and forefinger. "I went to town to try to find you a necklace for our six-month anniversary."

She wrinkled her nose, trying to think. He was right. Tomorrow would be exactly six months since they'd gotten married. She'd completely forgotten. "I'm so sorry," she said with a gasp. "Things have been so crazy, I must've completely forgotten."

He nodded. "I thought you had. I was at the jewelry store trying to find the perfect one when I got your text. I came home right after. But, look, I still want to do something nice for you. What if we go out of town for the weekend?"

She smiled. "Like a mini-vacation?"

"Yes. Exactly like a mini-vacation," he agreed. "We could use some alone time away from all of the chaos."

She leapt into his arms, kissing him softly through a laugh. "That sounds perfect." He kissed her back.

"It's settled, then," he said. "Now, we both need a bath, and then we can start packing."

She jumped down, hurrying toward the bathroom with his hand in hers. For a moment, the fight was forgotten. As were his instructions to stay away from the one person she suddenly found herself completely drawn to.

CHAPTER TWENTY

BRYANT

He'd almost ruined everything. Everything. His marriage. His happiness. His life. All for a girl that, at the end of the day, was nothing more than a fling. His attraction to her was purely physical. On the way to Myrtle Beach, he repeated those things over and over in his mind. He needed to focus on his marriage now. Fix what he'd broken with Harper, even if she didn't realize what he was doing.

He'd cut Tori out of his life and asked Harper to do the same. He couldn't let the two of them get around each other…who knows what secrets may be spilled.

More than that, he couldn't get the way Jason had been looking at Harper out of his mind. The guy was obviously attracted to her. If he hadn't come up at the exact moment he did, if he hadn't interrupted, who knows what could've happened?

He shook his head, trying to rid himself of the thoughts, and reached for Harper's hand. "I love you."

"I love you, too," she mused, smiling back at him. "I can't believe it's already been six months."

"Me either. Six amazing months. I think back to how we met...you were just this girl who dropped her laundry basket on the quad."

"And you were just a boy who held my panties before we'd even said hello," she said with a loud laugh. "Very forward of you."

"I think you mean very 'gentlemanly' of me," he said. "If it wasn't for me, you would've lost all of your clothes that day. I saved you from having to be naked."

"Well, the way I remember it, after we met, I was naked a lot more than I'd been before." She winked at him, and he let out a soft growl from deep in his throat. He released her fingers, letting his hand dance across her bare thigh, his fingers toying with the edge of her shorts.

"I really missed you."

She ran her fingers across his arm. "What are you talking about? I've been right here."

"I know," he said, "but it doesn't feel that way. I feel like we've lost touch."

"Why?" she asked, seeming upset.

"I don't know. But we're going to fix that this weekend." He kissed her knuckles. "We're going to get back to where we were."

She looked down, obviously upset. "I hadn't realized we'd gotten so far from there."

He nudged her with his elbow, trying to coax a smile. "Hey, I didn't say there was anything wrong with us. Especially not you. I just...I haven't been doing the right things."

"What do you mean?" she asked, and he realized the sentence had slipped from his mouth before he was ready.

"I just haven't been paying enough attention, I think." He tried to cover his tracks. "With our schedules so out of whack, it's been hard. But, I'm here now. We're here...and this is right where I want to be."

He swallowed, fighting back the tears that were stinging his eyes as he realized how true that was, and just how close he was to losing it all.

CHAPTER TWENTY-ONE

HARPER

That night, the couple lay in the hotel bed, cuddling in their quiet room. It had been a long day filled with amusement rides on the boardwalk, pigging out on funnel cakes and lemon shake ups, and coming back to the hotel to make love until they were both worn out.

"I'm glad we decided to come," Harper told her husband. "Today has been just what I needed." He nodded, his chin rubbing against her head, but didn't speak. "Bryant? Are you okay?" she asked, sitting up. He'd been strangely quiet since arriving back at the hotel, even seeming somewhat out of it during sex. Something was going on with him, that much she knew, but she just couldn't seem to pinpoint what it was.

"Yeah," he said calmly, letting out a sigh. "I'm fine, baby. Why?"

"You just seem off."

He kissed her forehead. "You know I love you, right?"

"I do." She propped herself up on her elbows. "Why do I feel like there's a 'but' coming?"

He shook his head. "No 'but.' It's just something I should let you know more often."

She smiled. "So, how's school going? We haven't talked about it much lately. Are your students still giving you a hard time?"

"Nah, not too bad. I mean, they're teenagers who generally suck by default, but it's getting better. Now that they know I won't put up with their shit."

"That's right," she teased, patting his chest. "Hey, about earlier today with Jason, I still feel really bad about everything—"

He pressed his lips into hers, ending her sentence. "You have nothing to feel bad about. I trust you."

"Are you sure?"

"More than anything. Look, I really just want to forget about them this weekend." *And the rest of my life, if I'm being honest.* "I'd rather it just be about us."

"You've got it," she said. "No more talking about them. Only us."

She paused slightly, knowing she must've been wrong, but before she put her head down on his chest again, she could've sworn she saw him wipe a tear from his eye.

CHAPTER TWENTY-TWO

HARPER

When the couple arrived back to their house on Sunday evening, sun-kissed and waterlogged, they were both aching to make their way into a familiar space. When they pulled into the drive, every hair on Harper's arms stood up. "Bryant," she whispered, her heart seizing in her chest.

His eyes followed her gaze, his jaw hanging open. "I see it."

The front door to their house stood wide open, freeing up passage to anyone who wanted to enter. Anyone who already had. "Should we call the police?"

He nodded, already pulling out his phone and dialing. "Do not get out of the car," he instructed, though he was stating the obvious. There was no way Harper was moving, not now, possibly not ever. Lancaster Mills was starting to feel anything but the small, safe town they'd believed it to be.

When he hung up the phone, letting her know that the police would be there in just a few minutes, he reached over and squeezed her hand. "It's probably just the wind," he assured her. "I'll bet when we shut the door, it didn't latch all the way."

"You didn't check it?" she demanded.

"Weren't you the last one out?" he asked, furrowing his brow.

Truth was, she couldn't remember, and at that point it didn't matter. "I don't know," she said. "Maybe we should go check with Tori and Jason. They could've seen something."

"No," he said. "Let's just stay in the car. The police will be here soon." He nodded his head toward the end of the road. "We should be here waiting when they arrive."

She nodded, feeling less than safe. What if someone was still in their house? What if they'd robbed them? As young newlyweds just starting out, it wasn't like they had many things of value, but the thought that their home had been invaded was terrifying. She sat, contemplating what could've been taken and waiting for the police car that eventually came.

She felt a bit safer as she watched the officers stepping from their car. Bryant climbed from his side, nodding at her to let her know it was okay to do the same. She did, meeting the officers in the middle.

"I'm Officer Casey," the first man greeted them. "This is my partner, Officer Glendale. So, you think you've been robbed?"

"We don't know," Bryant said. "We just arrived home from a vacation. We were only gone over the weekend, but when we got here, well…" He gestured toward the open front door to explain.

"You haven't gone inside yet, correct?"

"No we haven't," Bryant said. "We didn't know who could be in there."

The officers nodded in unison, reaching for their weapons. "You two get back into your car until we give you the all clear. We're going to do a quick perimeter check and go into the house. If we don't find anyone, we'll let you know it's safe to enter."

The couple did as instructed, watching as the cops radioed dispatch to let them know what was happening before heading toward the house. They sat in agonizing silence, watching one disappear into the house while the other went around the back, both guns raised. After a few moments, Officer Glendale came back around, waving for them to come in with a quick nod. Harper let out a sigh of relief she hadn't realized she'd been holding. "Oh, thank God." She felt cool tears filling her eyes as she walked around the car, taking Bryant's hand and preparing herself for the absolute worst.

This was why they had house insurance, after all. Things could be replaced. They walked up the front porch steps and into the living room, and she stared around in shock.

Not a single thing seemed out of place. Their flat screen television was still sitting on the entertainment center. The laptop was lying where she'd left it on the couch cushion. Nothing was ransacked or destroyed. Aside from a bit of dust and debris from the door being open, the house looked untouched.

"No one's here. Far as I can tell, it looks like the place is fine. You'll want to go check upstairs and make sure nothing's missing," Officer Casey told them. She could feel his frustration already. They'd wasted their time. She walked upstairs slowly, her husband close behind her, neither of them speaking. They walked through each room. Her jewelry, what little she owned, was still there. The desktop still remained on the office desk. Everything was the same. Nothing had been touched.

They walked back downstairs, Harper unable to hide her embarrassment for not actually being robbed, though she knew that was ridiculous. The officers must think they were crazy, and could she blame them? They'd acted so impulsively.

"We're so sorry," she offered as soon as she saw them.

"Everything's in place, then?" Officer Glendale asked, his arms folded across his chest.

"It seems to be," Bryant answered.

"Right," Officer Casey said. "Well, looks like maybe the door just didn't get latched all the way, then."

"I feel so stupid," Harper confessed. "I hate that we wasted your time."

"No," Casey said, "don't. That's what we're here for. Better safe than sorry. These old doors can be tricky, just try to jiggle the handle a little next time before you leave to be safe. You're lucky you guys didn't get animals in here."

Bryant nodded, reaching out to shake their hands. "Thanks, Officers. We really appreciate you coming out to check." With that, the two men left, saying a final goodbye as they made it out the door. Bryant turned to Harper, heaving a dramatic sigh. "Well, that's one way to come home, eh?"

She shook her head, unable to rid herself of the uneasy feeling. "Yeah. I could've sworn I shut the door though."

He hugged her. "Don't beat yourself up over it. At least we're both safe and nothing's missing."

She wrapped her arms around him, tucking her face into his chest and letting the tears of adrenaline fall. She'd been so worried, and now that the officers were gone, she finally allowed herself to feel it all. She lifted her head up, prepared to kiss her husband, and gasped.

"What is it?" he asked, turning around to see what had caught her eye.

"What the hell is that?" she demanded.

There, hanging off the kitchen chair was a red, lacy bra. If she had to guess, it was about two cup sizes larger than her own.

"I have no idea," Bryant said, though his voice had lost its power. "It's not yours?"

She walked over to the chair, staring at the bra. "You know it's not," she said hastily. "Why would this be here?"

"I have no idea," he said, swallowing hard. "It wasn't here when we left."

"So someone *was* here." She reached for her phone. "We need to call the police again."

He shook his head, seeming unsure. "I don't know. I mean, if we call them back…there's still not anyone here. What, we're just going to give them this bra? Tell them it was hanging on the chair and wasn't yours? I don't want to waste their time anymore."

"You heard them. This is their job," she insisted.

"DNA testing bras?"

"Bras that are in houses they don't belong in, yes. Why are you acting like I'm the crazy one here?"

He rubbed his forehead. "Look, if you want to call them, we can. All I'm saying is…when we tell them nothing's missing—still—but we think someone broke in and dropped off a bra, they're going to think we're insane."

She sighed, realizing how crazy it sounded. "You're right."

"We'll just throw it away and forget about it, okay? Nothing's missing. No one's here. It's probably just a misunderstanding."

"A misunderstanding?"

"Maybe Tori came over to do laundry and left it."

"Why would Tori be in our house doing laundry?" she demanded. "Besides, how do you even know it's hers?" It stung. She wouldn't deny that. The fact that he'd assume the bra that wouldn't fit his wife would be Tori's.

"I'm just guessing," he said stiffly. "Look, we're freaking out about nothing."

She shook her head. Was he right? It didn't feel like nothing. Someone had obviously been in her house. But, was it Tori? If she'd come over, Harper wouldn't mind, but why wouldn't she have shut the door? More than that, why would she have left her bra? She could go over and ask, she guessed, but that seemed weird.

Finally, she let out a sigh. There was no logical reason for any of it, and yet, she was realizing it was something she'd have to let go. At least for now. She grabbed a large Ziploc bag from the drawer, picking up the bra with her fingertips and easing it into the bag before shoving it into a junk drawer and going to scrub her hands. It felt dirty, somehow, but she didn't want to throw it out in case it was Tori's. She'd have to find a way to ask her.

She turned around. "You okay?" she asked. Her husband stood in the doorway, his eyes still as wide as when he'd pulled into the drive.

"Yeah," he said, blinking himself out of a trance. "It's just been a weird night."

She nodded as a cold chill ran over her. "Weird doesn't even begin to cover it."

CHAPTER TWENTY-THREE

HARPER

The next evening, Harper collapsed on the couch after work next to Bryant, propping her feet up on the coffee table. The old couch was so worn, it had a permanent place for her in the cushion, but they'd had it since they'd gotten their first place, and she couldn't bear to part with the many memories made on it: cramming for finals, pigging out after a hard day, hours of binge watching so many of their favorite shows, and so much more.

Bryant rested his head on hers, flipping through the channels aimlessly. "Did you see the new trailer for *The Walking Dead*?" he asked.

She laughed. "I saw where you shared it on Facebook this morning. So dang cool. I can't believe—" She stopped as a sharp rap at the door interrupted her. "Who is that?" she asked, sitting up.

The couple stood from the couch, and Bryant approached the door apprehensively. He looked through the beveled glass. "What the hell?" As he pulled open the door, Harper got a look at the person standing before them: a pizza delivery boy with a tower of pizza boxes in his outstretched arms. "Uh, what's this?" Bryant asked.

"Your pizzas," the boy answered, letting out a sigh as if to emphasize the fact that they were heavy. "This is eight fourteen, right?" He stepped back to look at the house number.

"Yeah, it is," Bryant said, shaking his head while still not taking the boxes. "But we didn't order any pizza."

"Well, it says you did," he said. "It's already paid for."

Bryant shook his head again. "I don't understand."

"Look, my boss isn't gonna let me leave unless you take the pizza."

"What kind are they?" Bryant asked, as if that mattered.

Finally, the boy set the pizzas on the ground. "I'm sorry, but there you go." He looked at the receipt on top of the box, comparing it once again with the house number. "I don't know who ordered them, but this is your address. Have a nice night. guys. I've got other deliveries." With that, he turned around, disappearing down the porch steps and back to the beat-up blue car in the driveway.

Bryant turned to look at Harper. "What the hell?" he repeated.

"I don't know," she said, trying to rub away the goosebumps that had appeared on her arms. "I guess bring them in."

"Seven pizzas?" he said, his voice filled with surprise. "What on earth are we going to do with seven pizzas? I don't even think we could eat seven pizzas in a week."

"Not before we get tired of it," Harper said, lifting a few boxes off the top of the stack. "Maybe you could take some of it to your classes tomorrow."

He nodded. "Yeah, m..ybe. Who would've sent it, though?"

"Maybe it's one of those 'pay it forward' things," she responded.

"Well, someone majorly paid it forward, then. I hope it's

not delivered to the wrong house. They'll be coming back and making us pay for it or something."

"I can't see how they could do that," Harper argued. "And it does have our address on it." She pointed to the receipt. "Strange." She opened the lid, letting out a gasp. "Well, that's weird. Mine has the pepperonis in the shape of a 'T' on it. Does yours have letters? Maybe it spells your name or something."

He lifted one lid, then another. "Yeah, letters. I have a…H, R, and…hmm," he opened his last box, "and A. What are the rest of yours?"

"I have a C, E, and another E, plus my T. What does it mean?" Harper asked, staring at the letters in confusion. "Surely it means something."

The couple stared at the letters, their heads bouncing from one side to the other as they studied the letters. Finally, Harper had solved it. "Cheater?" she asked. "It spells cheater."

Bryant frowned. "That can't be the only thing it spells." His face lit up. "It spells teacher, too!"

"Why would someone send us pizza with toppings spelling 'cheater' or 'teacher' though? Is it supposed to be a joke?" she asked, a sick feeling washing over her.

Bryant's face lit up suddenly, and he held up a finger. "I know who sent it."

"Who?" she demanded.

"A student in my class. I gave him detention today for cheating on his test. That's exactly it, this must be some kind of practical joke."

"Well, it isn't very funny," Harper said with a hand on her hip. "It's wasteful."

"I know," Bryant agreed. "I'll bring it to class tomorrow, like you said. In the meantime, looks like we're both off the hook for dinner tonight." He grabbed a slice, popping it into his mouth. "Come on, *Schitt's Creek* is getting ready to start."

She nodded, grabbing a piece and following suit. She'd give in and follow his lead, though she didn't completely buy his story. Something strange was going on, and each day, things just seemed to get weirder. She was determined to find out the truth, whether her husband wanted to or not.

CHAPTER TWENTY-FOUR

BRYANT

The next day, after Harper had left for work, Bryant headed straight for Tori's office. He was a mess. He had to confront her about the bra in his home. Her bra. The same bra she'd been wearing the day they'd had sex, and then about the pizzas last night. Even though he'd somewhat convinced Harper she was the one to leave the door unlatched, he knew it was him. But he'd told her he was sure if it was him, he'd shut it well. He wouldn't take the blame. It was locked when they'd left, he assured her. It had to be. Which meant Tori had to have picked the locks. Unless, he'd somehow forgotten to lock the back door. Unless they were somehow responsible for the mugging. They'd have the key, then. But that was crazy. All of this was absolutely preposterous. So many possibilities swam through his mind...none of them making any real sense. He had to put an end to it. And now.

He pulled into her parking lot, marching in the door with gusto. "Can I help you?" A petite, red headed receptionist greeted him from behind thick glasses.

"I need to see Tori."

"Doctor Fuller is with a patient right now. Do you have an appointment?"

"No," he said firmly. "But I need to see her. It'll just take a second. Can you tell her it's an emergency?"

The receptionist looked uncomfortable but eventually stood up and walked down a long hall. After a moment, she reappeared. "She'll be right out."

He walked toward the chairs, but didn't sit. He was too nervous. He paced around, waiting to see her, planning what he'd say when he did.

"Bryant?" Her honey-like voice called to him from across the room, and he spun around. Her lips parted slightly, her eyes locked on his, and she tilted her head up just a bit, looking confused. "What are you doing here?"

"We need to talk," he said, walking past her and to the office. She didn't stop him, following closely behind and shutting the door after they'd entered. She didn't speak at first, her eyes sizing him up as her arms folded across her chest.

She spoke with a slight smirk on her face. "What can I do for you?"

"Cut the shit, Tori. I know what you're doing, and it ends now."

"I don't know what you're talking about."

"You're mad because I called it off, and now you're stalking me."

She scoffed, holding her hands up in front of her chest. "Wait, hold on, *stalking you?* Are you kidding me? No, baby, I'm not stalking you."

"Don't call me 'baby.' Don't call me anything. I told you I wanted you to stay away from me, and then you go and break into my house. What kind of sick person are you? You left your bra for my wife to find? Are you trying to get us caught? Is that it? You want her to know? 'Cause if that's your plan, I'd rather you just tell her now than continue toying with me."

"You want her to know about us?"

He sucked in a breath, pressing his lips together. "No, of course not. But I can't live like this, either."

"Bryant, I honestly have no idea what you're talking about."

"Well, if you don't, then how do you explain your red bra at my house?"

"Is that where it is? I've been looking for it, but I have no idea how it'd get there."

"You're lying," he insisted. "You're playing games. Fucking with my head because I hurt you. I'm sorry, okay? I never meant to—"

"Let me stop you right there," she said, stepping forward. In her heels, she was just as tall as him, her blue-green eyes lining up with his brown ones perfectly. "You didn't hurt me. Am I pissed? Yeah, a little bit. I don't do rejection. I never have. What you did...cheating on your wife and then trying to make me feel bad about it—"

"You cheated on your husband, too—"

"*I wasn't finished,*" she screeched. "What you did was wrong, but I've moved on. I'm happy. I can have anyone I want. I can do anything I want." She took a step even closer, her warm breath on his face. "So, you choosing to walk away...well, you just beat me to it. Honestly, I would've gotten bored with you, anyway. But let me tell you what's not going to happen...you coming to my office. Never again, hear me? Never. You don't wanna see me? Fine. Two can play that game, Bryant. But if you wanna do this, you'll start a war. Stay the hell out of my office and out of my life, or I promise you, you'll be sorry. Now," she said, lowering her gaze to his lips so quickly he was sure she was going to go in for a kiss, "get out."

CHAPTER TWENTY-FIVE

HARPER

On her way out to her car that evening, Tori found her in the parking lot. "Harper!" she called, waving a quick hand over her head before she saw her.

"Hey," Harper said. "Everything okay?" She was honestly shocked to see her. It had been a while since the last time she tracked her down at work.

"Yeah, everything's fine. Actually, I felt like I should apologize to you."

"Apologize for what?" she asked.

"For the bra. Bryant mentioned you guys found it at your house. Truth is, I'd come over to see if you knew anything about sewing. The strap is starting to wear down, and it's my favorite. I'm useless with a needle and thread on anything except skin, but I thought you might be able to help. Anyway, I didn't mean to leave it there. When I came over, your door was open, and I laid it down to go check and see if you guys were home or okay or whatever. I guess I got startled and left it there. I'm really sorry again. I didn't mean to upset you."

"Oh, it's okay," Harper said. "Honestly. But...did you say the door was open when you arrived? When was that?"

"Um, Saturday night, I guess it would've been."

"Did you shut it back when you left?"

"Well, of course. I didn't have a way to lock it, because I don't have a key and we don't have your numbers, but we kept an eye on it. I just assumed it didn't latch correctly. Those doors can be tricky," she said, her eyes narrowing.

"Yeah, I guess so. It was back open when we came home."

"What?" Tori gasped, covering her mouth. "I know it was shut when I left. Do you think someone broke in?"

"If they did, they didn't take anything," Harper said. "You never saw anyone come by?"

"Never," Tori vowed. "That's terrifying."

"Have you guys ever had any trouble at your place?"

"Nope," Tori said, "but we have a security system, just in case. Never had any issues, though. The wind did get kind of bad Sunday, so maybe that was it."

"Maybe," Harper agreed. "Anyway, you didn't have to come all the way out here just to tell me that."

She smiled. "I didn't want you to be mad at me. And, confession, that wasn't the only reason." She pressed her lips together firmly, her eyes darting back and forth between Harper's. "I wanted to make sure we were okay, after the other day."

"What do you mean?"

She rolled her eyes. "Look, it didn't mean anything to me, but I know you're pretty inexperienced. The kiss wasn't a...I wasn't *coming on* to you. It was just harmless fun."

"Oh," Harper waved her hand, trying to play much cooler than she felt, "of course. No, did you think that bothered me? I know it was no big deal."

"Okay, good," Tori said, resting her hand on Harper's shoulder. "Good. I'd hate to think you've been avoiding me."

"Not at all. Things have just been crazy, you know?"

"Definitely," she said, drawing out the word. She offered

her a pouty smile. "Anyway, I've got to run. We'll catch up soon, okay? What do you think, drinks on Friday?"

"Uh, sure."

"Perf," she said, leaning down and kissing both her cheeks as if they were stars. "I'll catch you soon."

Harper nodded, waving at her, though her back was already turned. When she climbed into the car, she dialed Bryant's number, waiting to hear his voice over the speaker before she pulled out. "Hey," she greeted him. "Did you go talk to Tori today?"

"What?" he asked, sounding distant. He must've had her on speakerphone.

"Tori. She came by my work. She was apologizing for leaving her bra at the house."

"She was?" He was back to the speaker then, his voice much louder.

"Yeah, didn't she tell you?"

He cleared his throat. "Well, I mean, yeah, but I didn't know she was coming to see you."

"She just wanted to say sorry. Apparently she'd wanted me to fix a loose thread on it."

"What?" he asked. "Why?"

"I guess it's her favorite bra, and she's useless with sewing clothes. Even though she sews skin for a living, so that seems kind of odd."

"She doesn't really seem like the 'repair what's broken' type. I just assumed she'd get something new."

"Some people are sentimental about their stuff," she said. "Anyway, she invited me to dinner Friday night. Do you want to come? I could see about you and Jason joining us." She didn't tell him she was only inviting him to make herself feel more comfortable. The thought of being alone again with Tori terrified her, but she felt compelled to say yes. Maybe being in the South was making her a nicer person, or maybe she just wanted to figure out what *things* Jason was *seeing* that she wasn't.

"What? No. I thought we were going to stay away from them?"

"Why?" she demanded. "I thought we were okay now? Tori and Jason are our friends. I don't want to have to avoid them and make things awkward." She knew the awkwardness would all fall on her. Bryant had a way of pleasing everyone, while she accepted the brunt of the responsibility for letting people down. It had always been the dynamic of their relationship. She was the bad news deliverer, the canceller of plans, and the holder of all 'maybe next times.'

"I don't want to hang out with them, Harp. They aren't like us."

"What's that supposed to mean?"

"Come on, you know what I mean. They're nothing like the friends we've had before."

"I mean, they're a little older. Richer, for sure. But, so what? They like us, we like them. I'm not saying we need to be best friends, but there's no reason we can't spend time with them. The more we get to know them, the more comfortable the whole situation will be."

"I said no," Bryant said firmly.

"You aren't the boss of me, dude," she said through gritted teeth. "You don't have to go if you don't want. But I am. I actually like Tori, and I don't want to hurt either of their feelings."

"Fine, whatever. I'll go."

"Don't do me any favors," she said hatefully. "You've been acting so weird lately."

He let out a sigh. "We'll just talk about it later, okay?"

"Yeah, fine." She hung up the phone without saying goodbye. "But I'm still going," she said, long after he was gone.

CHAPTER TWENTY-SIX

HARPER

When Harper arrived at home, Bryant was just coming out of the shower. He ran a towel through his hair on the way out of the bathroom, greeting her casually. "Hey babe," he said.

"Hey," she told him. "Have a good day?" She wanted to wait and see if he'd bring up the fight, though she was sure he wouldn't. Bryant was never one for confrontation. He'd much rather brush things under the rug than ever have to discuss them.

"Yeah, it was fine. How was yours?" He walked back from the laundry room, offering her a glass of white wine and a kiss.

"Thank you," she said, taking the glass. "It was okay. I'm just exhausted. My feet are killing me."

"Sit down," he said, taking her bag. "Hey, did you adjust the speed on the shower head?"

"What?"

"It was on full force when I got in. I usually keep it on the middle setting. Do you like the highest?"

She shook her head, taking another drink. "I didn't touch the shower head. You must've."

"No," he said, hanging her bag up on the coat rack. "It wasn't me."

"Well, it had to be you," she said adamantly, "because I don't ever pay attention to the settings."

He stared at the television, appearing to be thinking before inhaling deeply. "I'll bet you did it by accident when you cleaned it Saturday."

"You haven't showered since then?"

He frowned, propping his feet up next to hers. "I just probably didn't notice. No big deal."

She nodded, resting her head on his chest. "What's for dinner?" she asked. "I'm starving."

"I put a tenderloin in," he said. "I figured we'd do salads with it. I think I gained ten pounds in Myrtle Beach."

She patted his stomach. "I love you just the way you are," she teased, wrinkling her nose at him.

He kissed her head. "Do you ever think about going back?"

"Going back?" she asked.

"To Chicago. Do you miss it?"

She looked up at him, surprised by the question. "Of course I do. More than anything. Why?"

"I've just been thinking about it lately. I don't know. I miss the city. I mean, Lancaster Mills is fine, but it doesn't feel like home."

"We only just got here, Bryant," she told him. "No place could feel like home just yet. Did you feel at home in Chicago a month after you moved there?"

"No, of course not. I just don't want you to be homesick."

"I know," she said, "and I love you for that. But, I'm okay here. Really, I am. Of course I miss home. And my family. But, we're okay here, you know? We're starting somewhere fresh. Plus your job is great, and I get along with the people I work with." She nodded her head firmly, narrowing her eyes at him. "Life is good here, okay? Don't worry about me."

He kissed her again. "I just want you to be happy," he told her, their foreheads pressed together.

"Wherever you are...I'm happy."

CHAPTER TWENTY-SEVEN

HARPER

Harper's eyes shot open, the noise from her dreams carrying over into the dark night around her. She sat up in bed and stared around the moonlit room. What on earth was going on?

In the distance, she could distinctly hear music playing. It was a song she didn't recognize, though it reminded her of the older music her mother had loved when she was a kid. She looked over at her husband, sleeping peacefully despite the impending threat in their home.

Could the music be coming from outside, though? Her head was still filled with sleep, so it was possible she wasn't thinking straight. She lifted the covers, nudging him hurriedly.

"Bryant!" she whispered heatedly. "Bryant wake up!"

"Hm?" he asked, rolling over and wiping his chin. He sat halfway up. "What is—"

"Shhhh!" she quieted him. "Do you hear that?"

He was quiet for a moment, but then his face grew serious, and she knew she wasn't imagining it. "What is that? Is someone in our house?" he asked.

"I don't…I don't know." Her rapid breathing was making it increasingly hard to talk. "Should we call the police?" She reached over to the nightstand where her phone was supposed to be and froze. "Bryant…"

"Mine's gone, too," he said, the panic present in his tone more than ever. "Wait here. I'm going to go see what's going on."

"I'm not letting you go by yourself," she said angrily, grabbing hold of his arm. "What if there's a robber?"

He disappeared into the closet, grabbing the baseball bat from the corner. "I've got this. If I don't come back—"

"Don't say that—"

"If I don't, Harper, you hide until you absolutely can't anymore."

She shook her head. "I'm not letting you go by yourself, Bryant. I'll go with you."

He sighed as the music continued to play, its doo-wop tones taunting them. "Fine. But stay behind me."

She nodded, taking hold of his shirt as they walked down the hall and then the stairs cautiously. Her heart thudded so loudly in her chest and ears, she was sure it would drown out the music eventually.

As they made their way down the stairs, the music grew louder and more clear. They were on the right track. Closing in on the source. But what could it be? If someone had broken in, why would they turn on music to alert them to their presence? It didn't make any sense. Her thoughts raced, thinking of every dark possibility as they came into the living room. They looked around, the music playing so loudly it drowned out any sound throughout the rest of the house. It was as if they were at a nightclub and they were the only patrons.

Following the sound, they tiptoed toward the kitchen, Bryant with the bat raised over his head and Harper with tears in her eyes as she clung to his shirt for dear life. She'd seen enough horror movies to know that at some point, their intruder was going to end up behind them, and so she kept checking over her shoulder, picturing the face-off that she was sure would ultimately lead to their death.

The house looked untouched. Like the night after the Myrtle Beach trip, if not for the obvious signs that someone was in the house, or had been in the house, she would think she'd imagined it. Their electronics remained where they'd left them. *Except for their phones.*

As they walked into the kitchen, Bryant's bat lowered. "What the fuck?"

She peered around his shoulder, staring at what had caught his eye. There, resting on their small dining room table, were their phones, laying side by side and face up. He reached for his slowly, touching the home button and watching it light up to reveal a screen from the Apple Music store. According to the screen, they were listening to "Goodnight Sweetheart" by MC6 A Cappella. Bryant's shaking thumb pushed the pause button, and the house instantly fell silent as the two lines transformed into a triangle on the screen.

"What the *fuck?*" he repeated.

She shook her head, but she couldn't summon any words from her throat.

"Hello?" he called. For a moment, she thought he was being smart with her, but she quickly realized he was calling it out in general, daring their intruder to appear. She looked around the house, her blood running cold as they stood in silence, waiting for anyone to make a sound.

After a moment, Bryant sighed. "Did we leave our phones down here?"

"No," she insisted. "At least...I don't think so."

"We definitely didn't leave them blasting that music," he said. "I've never even heard that song."

"Me either," she admitted, rubbing her hands over her biceps in an attempt to warm the cold chills that ran deep below the surface.

"Should we still call the police?" he asked, his eyebrows raised.

She knew he was thinking the same thing she was. That if they did call the police...*again*...they needed to have something more to tell them than the fact that someone had broken in, taken their phones, downloaded a song, and played it. They had no proof. No way of knowing anything had happened. But that didn't stop the fear that had gripped her internal organs with icy fingers.

"Maybe the house is haunted," she said, half-joking, but with true horror in her voice.

"We had to have left the phones, right? Maybe some weird update came through and caused a glitch?"

"Updates usually wait until the phones are plugged in..."

Bryant bit his lip. "What do you think, then? What could've happened? I really think we should call the cops."

She could barely force her words out as every possibility ran through her head. "I agree. I just...what will we say?"

His expression fell from terrified to hopeless as he stared at his phone. "I have no idea. No one has my passcode, either. Or my thumbprint."

Harper shook her head as a chilling vision of the intruder lifting their thumbs in their sleep to access the phones. What would they have had access to? Everything. Too much. Their entire lives were on their phones.

"I don't want to look stupid again," she admitted, feeling foolish. Their lives were more important. She knew that. But were they in danger? Now that the initial adrenaline had calmed a bit, she wasn't so sure.

"Do you think one of us could've been sleepwalking?"

She shrugged. "It's as good a theory as any, I guess."

Truth was, no theory made any sense, and they both knew that. But what could they say?

"What should we do, Harp?" he asked, rubbing her shoulders. "You tell me."

She swallowed. "Coffee. Let's just…let's make coffee."

"Coffee?" he asked, his voice filled with confusion.

"Well, I'm not planning to sleep anymore tonight." Her eyes met his. "Are you?"

"No," he admitted. "Definitely not."

CHAPTER TWENTY-EIGHT

HARPER

A week later, Harper lay on the couch, sipping on ginger ale. The incident with their phones had been virtually forgotten. Nothing appeared to be touched except for the new addition to Bryant's song library, and nothing further had happened to cause them concern. But now she was sick, and that seemed to have taken precedence over any worry. She rubbed her stomach, cursing the day she'd ever decided to work in a hospital where the flu ran rampant.

Her phone chimed with a text message, and it took all of her strength to reach it on the table. She stared at the message from Bryant.

Checking in. You feeling any better?

She replied slowly, her fingers moving across the phone's screen. **No...need more ginger ale and saltines on your way home.**

You got it.

She tossed the phone down beside her, rolling over and trying to focus on the television, which featured some housewives show that annoyed her. The remote was too far out of reach for her to change it, and she didn't dare sit up, so she tried to suffer through. After a while, even the movement from the screen seemed to make her more nauseous, and so she rolled back over, placing the pillow over her head. This was her third day with the bug, and she was sure she'd never been so miserable.

A knock sounded on the door, and she couldn't find the strength to get up. Instead, she lay there, listening to the knocking and praying it would go away quickly. Whoever it was, they didn't need anything as badly as she needed not to move.

A third knock came, and she groaned loudly, realizing they weren't going to go away. She tried to sit up, but felt her stomach lurch from the movement and grabbed the trash can just in time to empty the measly contents of her stomach again.

"Harper?" She heard his voice through the door. "Are you okay?" It was Jason, and she was mortified that he was listening to her getting sick loudly, though she couldn't seem to quiet the retching. Suddenly, he was jiggling the door handle, and before she knew it, he was inside. "Oh my god," he said, rushing in and to her side in an instant. His arms were around her shaking shoulders. "Can I get you something?" he asked, when her stomach finally calmed and she wiped her mouth with a tissue from the box.

"Water," she croaked, blotting the corners of her mouth and trying not to cringe at the thought of what she must look like.

He nodded, walking toward the kitchen quickly. She could hear him opening and shutting the cabinets as he searched for the one with the glasses before he finally turned on the water and returned to her side. "Here you go," he said, handing her the glass of room-temperature water. "Is it the flu?"

She shook her head. "I guess so. Perks of working with the public, right?"

He smiled, giving her a sly wink. "I wouldn't know. Perks of being a writer."

"Do you need something?" she asked, feeling almost instantly better as she stood, desperate to get her bag of vomit as far away from her gorgeous neighbor as possible.

"I was just coming to check on you. Tori said you were sick on Friday, and she stopped by the hospital today, but they told her you'd called in," he said, watching her walk down the hall. She stopped in front of the bathroom sink and ran a wet hand through her hair, patting her pale cheeks. She grabbed her spare pink toothbrush from the drawer, brushing vigorously to get the terrible taste out of her mouth. When she was done, she sighed. There wasn't much she could do to improve her haggard appearance in the moments she had before it would be obvious that's what she was doing.

"Oh, yeah," she said, rubbing her stomach as she turned to walk back toward him. "I can't seem to kick this. Actually, it's probably a bad idea for you to be here. I'd hate for you to get sick."

"Too late now," he said simply. "Do you want some soup? Is there anything I can help you with?"

She crossed her arms. "I'm okay," she assured him. "Really, I am. It seems like once I've gotten sick, I'm usually okay for a few hours until it hits me again. Weirdest sickness ever."

He nodded. "Well, let me make you some broth to drink. That way you can rest."

"Why are you being so nice to me?" she asked.

"I like taking care of people," he said simply. "Especially people I care about."

"You care about me?" she asked, feeling her pale cheeks burn red.

"I do," he said. "You guys are our friends. I'd hope you'd do the same for either of us."

She nodded. "Of course we would. I hated that I couldn't come out with Tori on Friday."

"To be honest, we thought you might just be blowing her off, but I see now you really are sick," he said with a shrug. "Good to know."

"Why would I be blowing you off?" she asked, taking a step toward him.

He didn't move, staring straight at her. "Because of what I said earlier. About knowing things, observing things."

"Yeah, what was that about?"

"I just...I think your husband is attracted to Tori," he said with a wince. "I don't mean for that to sound callous, and honestly, you've probably noticed it, too."

She frowned because she had. And how could she blame him? "He would never act on it, if that's what you're worried about. Besides that, Tori has...*you*. Why would she ever ruin that with Bryant?" she asked. He let out a soft laugh under his breath.

"Well, he must be a catch to have gotten you," he said finally. Her stomach knotted up at his words, and she was unable to meet his eyes.

After a moment, she cracked a smile. "Was that a line?"

"Just the truth." He shrugged, brushing a piece of hair behind her ear.

She swallowed, looking down and retucking the hair. "Either way, I'm not nearly as much of a catch as your wife."

He furrowed his brow, lifting her chin so she was forced to look at him. "I disagree."

She looked up from underneath her lashes, her hands shaking. "W-what do you mean?"

"I'm just saying, look, Tori's beautiful, no question. And she's not a bad person. But those things alone don't make someone a catch. You'll see how it is once you two have been married long enough. Eventually, even someone you thought was a diamond begins to lose their shine."

"Well, that's terrifying."

"It doesn't mean we don't love each other. It just means our love is different now. We can both appreciate beautiful people without worrying about it hurting our marriage."

"What are you saying?" she asked, taking a step back. She grabbed hold of a piece of her hair, twisting it around a shaking finger.

He let out a sigh. "I'm sorry. I'm freaking you out. Forget I said anything." He hurried into the kitchen. "Now, do you have chicken broth?"

She nodded her head toward the pantry. "Jason, are you saying Tori is attracted to Bryant, too?"

He walked over, pulling out the box of broth and opening the cabinets to search for a pan before he turned around. "Yeah, I think so." He waved his hand dismissively. "But it's not anything serious."

"Does he know?" she asked, her throat suddenly dry, stomach in a knot. She felt like she was going to be sick again as anger bubbled through her.

He didn't look her way immediately, instead turning on the burner and pouring the broth into a pan. When he turned around, his eyes were soft. "You'd have to ask him about that."

"But you think he does. That much is obvious."

He rubbed the nape of his neck. "I think...I think that my wife is far from discreet."

"So, you think she's going to act on it."

"I'd say she already has, Harper, but I don't know that for sure. I'm just guessing."

She swallowed. "Bryant wouldn't do anything. He

wouldn't cheat on me." She was trying to convince herself just as much as she was him. "He loves me."

He nodded. "I have no doubt that he does," he said simply. "I'm only saying…it's possible to love someone with all of your heart and still be attracted to other people."

"We aren't like that," she said, feeling her anger growing. "I'd like you to leave, please," she said. "Now."

He took a step toward her as she stepped back. "I didn't mean to upset you," he said, reaching for her arm. She jerked it away. "I'm really sorry, Harper. Honestly, I am."

"I'd like you to leave, Jason," she repeated.

He let out a sigh, but his arm finally fell to his side and his lips formed a thin line. He ducked his head down, walking past her. "I'm really sorry," he said, shutting the door behind him as he disappeared.

With hot, angry tears in her eyes, Harper hurried to the couch and grabbed her phone. She dialed Bryant's phone number from memory with shaking hands, watching as his name appeared on her screen before placing it to her ear.

"Hello?" he answered quickly, his voice low. She could hear the commotion in the background, and she knew he must be in class.

"I need you to come home," she insisted. "Now."

"What is it? Are you sick again?"

"Just come home, Bryant," she said, tired of keeping the tears at bay as she finally allowed them to fall.

"Harper?" he asked, seeming to realize she was crying. "Sweetheart, what is it?"

"Now," she begged. "Please, please come home now."

"I'll be there in twenty minutes," he promised, hanging up the phone without saying goodbye. Within seconds, she was grabbing the trash can and allowing her stomach to empty once again.

WHEN BRYANT ARRIVED AT HOME, he rushed into the room, his hair frazzled. "What is it?" he asked, eyes wide. "What happened?"

She sat up on the couch, staring at him with a horrified expression. "I need to ask you something," she said, wiping her eyes. "And I need you to be completely honest with me."

He froze in place, and she could swear his color fell two shades lighter. "Okay," he said, his voice barely above a whisper.

"Are you attracted to Tori?" she asked, crossing her arms and watching as his worried expression grew terrified.

"W-what? No! Of course not. No. Why would you think that? No! Babe, of course not." He spit the words out as fast as they would come, his head shaking incessantly.

"You're lying," she said, and they both knew she was right. She stood up, her eyes narrowing at him. "I know that you are."

"What did she say to you?" he asked.

She inhaled sharply at his almost-confession. That's what that was, right? His words told her all she needed to know. "What do you think she told me?"

He looked away, seeming to be contemplating his next move. When he looked back up, his jaw was tight and his eyes had grown watery. "I'm so sorry," he told her. She wanted to go to him, her automatic response when he showed any sign of vulnerability, but she couldn't. She had to stand firm here. She had to know the truth. The whole truth.

"You're sorry?" she asked. "For what, exactly?" She was trying to seem like she knew more than he did, and he was trying to determine exactly how much she did know. Bryant was an open book, his expressions so easy for her to read after so long together.

"I love you," he whispered.

"Bryant, you aren't getting out of this."

"I love you," he said again, stepping toward her and taking both of her hands in his. "I need you to hear that. I wanted to tell you what I did. What *we* did. It was stupid. A mistake. I never should've done it. It wasn't planned. It wasn't even entirely intentional. But, I still did it. I'll never forgive myself. I can't say I blame you if you never forgive me, either. But I do love you, Harper. Only you. Tori and I...it was a huge mistake. I never want to see her again. I want to be with you. Being with her, it only confirmed what I knew about us."

Tears began falling more freely, and she dropped his hands, unable to form words. She closed her eyes, trying desperately to pull herself together. "You...you slept with her?"

His eyes darted in between hers, and he seemed to realize his mistake. "You didn't know?"

She shook her head. "Jason said she was attracted to you. That he thought you were attracted to her, too."

"How would he know that? Wait a minute, why was Jason—"

She turned on her heel, storming into the kitchen with Bryant close behind. "Don't you dare! Don't you *dare* ask me what he was doing here. You have no right. None. You're a cheater and a liar and I hate you! I hate you!" she screamed, slamming the coffee mug she'd grabbed down onto the counter so hard it shattered.

He moved to pick it up, but she stepped in front of the mess. "Don't touch it. Get out of my sight, Bryant. I don't...I can't stand to look at you."

"I want to talk about this. I want to work things out. I don't want to lose you," he begged, his eyes filling with more tears.

"*GET OUT!*" she bellowed, pointing her finger toward the

doorway for emphasis. Every part of her body shook with adrenaline, and if he didn't get out of her sight that instant, she was sure she would hurt him. She sank to the ground as he backed out of the room, and she heard his footsteps headed upstairs. It was only when she heard the bedroom door close that she openly wept, crying both for the part of herself and the dream life she'd lost in the same day.

CHAPTER TWENTY-NINE

BRYANT

He was an idiot. A moron. A complete and utter imbecile. With each passing hour—each passing day —that he couldn't get Harper to speak to him, the truth grew louder in his head. He had become a man he hated and, in turn, lost the woman he loved.

He wasn't giving up. He would fight for her. He would fight for their marriage. But, he couldn't blame her if she blew him off. If the tables were turned, would he do anything differently? If she'd cheated on him? Likely not. It was a pain he knew well. Before Harper, his last girlfriend had cheated on him, and it still hurt to think about. Not to mention the fact that he'd watched his own mother grieve month after month over his father's indiscretions.

He hurried down the stairs as fast as his legs would move. He'd been late for work every day since their argument, but he couldn't bear to face Harper in the mornings. He didn't want to upset her any further. So, he holed up in the office where he'd blown up the air mattress to sleep. Every morning, he'd wait until he heard the front door shut, alerting him that she was gone, before he'd begin his morning routine.

So, as he rushed out the door, swinging his keys in his hand, his coffee sloshing as he ran, he cursed aloud as he saw what was awaiting him.

"Damn! You've got to be kidding me," he said, kicking the pavement underneath his feet. All four tires on the silver car had been slashed. He walked forward, trying to examine them closer. Sure enough, there was a long gash in each of the tires. *"Seriously?"* he cried loudly, pulling out his phone to send a quick text to the school's secretary to let her know he'd be late. He didn't bother calling the police, knowing it must've been Harper. Instead, he called a tow truck and stormed back inside.

Maybe it was a sign of progress, that she was at least acting out in her anger. For the past three days, it had been nothing but the silent treatment. Now she was communicating with him, even if it wasn't in a positive way. He'd take what he could get.

WHEN HARPER ARRIVED home that night, Bryant had the house cleaned top to bottom. He'd cooked steak with asparagus and had it waiting—hot and ready—on the table. She walked into the house, her purse weighing her down, hair falling from her bun, and looked around.

"What's this?" she asked, her face twisted in confusion.

"I, um," he hurried to her side, taking her purse from her and setting it down, "I thought maybe you'd be ready to talk now."

"Why would you think that? Wait, did you clean the house?" She glanced toward the kitchen.

"Yes. I did. I finished all the laundry and even scrubbed the bathtub and the floors."

She crossed her arms. "You've been busy."

"I have," he said. "And it's not nearly enough, but...I'm hoping it's a start."

"A start?"

"A start to...fixing us."

She let out a sarcastic laugh. "What? You thought you could fold a few loads of laundry and suddenly we'd be fine?"

"Of course not," he assured her. "That's not what I'm saying, but after I missed work today, instead of just being mad at you, I spent the day trying to prove to you how sorry I am. Shouldn't that count for something?"

"What are you talking about? You missed work? You can't blame me because you've been hiding out in that office every morning." She wagged a finger at him, shaking her head firmly. Her upper lip was curling, a sure sign she was furious.

"I haven't been *hiding out*, and that's not what I meant. But my tires? Really, Harper? I know you're mad, but we aren't made of money. That was six hundred dollars out of our savings."

"What are you talking about?" she asked, touching her chest. "What was?"

"My tires," he repeated, trying to understand the confused look on her face. "You slashed my tires this morning...didn't you?"

"Are you kidding me?" she screamed, rushing to the door. "Of course I didn't slash your tires."

"The car's in the shop," he said, explaining why the driveway was empty. "You didn't notice it wasn't here when you pulled in?"

"I just assumed you were visiting your girlfriend," she snarked, but continued before he could argue. "When were your tires slashed?"

"This morning before I could leave for work. I just assumed you did it."

Bewilderment filled her face as she turned to stare at him.

"You seriously think I'm that stupid? Why would I slash your tires?" She paused. "I know *why* I would, but come on, Bryant. Give me a little credit, will you? I'm not insane."

He shook his head. "You mean you didn't do it?"

"Of course I didn't do it!" she exclaimed, then looked back out the door. "So, who did?"

"Some kid, I guess," he said, his throat dry. "Who else could it have been?" When she didn't answer right away, he placed a hand on her shoulder. "I'm sorry." He didn't bother to explain for what, and honestly, he wasn't sure he could put into words just what he was apologizing for, but she seemed to understand.

"We don't have six hundred dollars sitting around. That money was supposed to go to pay off the credit card we put the U-Haul on."

"I know," he said. "We'll just have to keep saving. It's going to be okay."

"I'll see if I can work some doubles next week. Savannah's been out sick, it should be okay."

"I don't want you to do that," he said, tugging gently at her shoulders so she'd turn around.

"Well, I didn't want you to cheat on me," she said softly, avoiding his gaze. "I guess neither of us get what we want here." With that, she walked away with no power left in her voice.

CHAPTER THIRTY

HARPER

Harper stared into the long mirror on the back of the bathroom door, examining her body. The stomach bug she'd managed to endure for more than two weeks was causing her to lose weight pretty drastically. Add that to an illicit affair confession, and she was practically withering away. Though she would've once been glad to hear she'd dropped a few pounds, the curves she loved were disappearing with the excess weight. She'd gone past the goal weight she'd had since college days ago, and she was still losing.

Bryant knocked on the door hesitantly. "Hey, are you okay?" he asked through the wood, and she pulled her shirt down quickly.

"Yeah," she said, opening the door. "Need something?"

"I just need to get to the alcohol. I cut my hand on the box opener."

"Box opener?" she asked. "Why did you need the box opener?" She followed him over to the sink, where he attempted to wash out the gaping cut on his palm.

"I got a package," he said, opening the cabinet above him.

"It's down here," she told him, opening the bottom drawer and pulling the clear plastic bottle out. He reached for it, but she took his hand. "I'll do it. Hold still." He nodded, wincing. He'd never been very good with blood. "You can look away if you need to," she said with a soft laugh.

"Thank you," he told her, and she was sure it wasn't going over either of their heads that this was the first time she'd touched her husband in nearly two weeks. She poured the alcohol over his wound, rubbing her fingers over his skin to wipe away the blood. She missed this. His touch. Him. She missed feeling his skin against hers. And yet, as she stared down into his palms, she couldn't help picturing those same palms caressing Tori. What places had those hands explored? The hands that were only meant for her.

With tears stinging her eyes, she dropped his hand, setting the bottle down and rushing from the room without a word.

"Harper, wait!" he called, and she heard his heavy foot-steps approaching her.

"Please, just don't," she said, stopping dead in the living room. "What is all this?" she asked, staring at the pile of magazines and letters sitting on top of a brown box on the coffee table.

"The mail," he said, trying to dismiss it. "What happened?"

She walked to the pile. "Why do we have so much? What did you order?"

"I don't know. I assumed you ordered it."

She picked up the box. "But it's addressed to you. All of it. These letters…donation requests, subscriptions we never signed up for. *Playboy*," she said, holding up the magazine, "really?"

"It wasn't me!" he insisted, taking the magazines from her and tossing them into the trash for emphasis. "I swear it wasn't. I get my porn online like a normal person," he said, nudging her. A joke that maybe would've warranted a chuckle from her before only stung more.

"Or from next door," she whispered, though she wasn't sure he'd heard. She picked up the box cutter from the floor, noticing the specks of blood on the hardwood that she'd have to clean up soon, and slid it across the tape sealing up the box. She opened the box quickly, reaching in and pulling out the pink silk teddy inside. She turned to look at him, unable to keep the hurt expression from her face. It was clearly a size too big for her, especially in the chest. "What's this?"

His jaw dropped, staring at the lingerie. "Harper, I didn't." He held his hands up in front of his chest. "You have to know I wouldn't."

"I don't know what you would do anymore, Bryant," she said firmly, slamming the lingerie back into the box. She picked up the magazines, their fronts clad with women in bathing suits, and the countless letters asking them to donate to this cause and that, and tossed them all in the trash. "I don't know what's going on, but this is not okay."

"I didn't do any of this," he repeated firmly. "Now it's you who must think I'm stupid."

"I don't think you're stupid," she told him. "I'm just...I don't understand what's happening."

"It has to be Tori," he said, scratching his head.

"But...why? Why would she do this? What has she got to gain from it all?"

"Maybe she's angry that I ended it."

"Was there something to end?" she asked, swallowing.

"I mean, you know what I mean."

She nodded, folding her arms across her chest in a shiver. "Please just get rid of it," she said finally, turning to walk away.

"Can we just talk? *Please?* I'm doing all I know to do here," he said.

She spun on her heel, her finger pointed at him. *"All you know to do?* All you know to do? Seriously, you did not just say that to me, Bryant. Maybe, I don't know," she shrugged sarcastically, "maybe you should've done what you *knew to do* long before you were sliding up her skirt."

"I've said I'm sorry, Harper," he told her, his voice soft.

"Yeah, you have," she said. "But sorry doesn't fix it."

"What will?"

"I don't know."

"Well, where does that leave us?"

She thought for a moment. "I don't have that answer yet, Bryant. If that's not enough for you, then I don't know what to tell you."

"So, what am I supposed to do?"

"Whatever you want," she said with a shrug before turning back toward the hallway. "You're getting pretty good at that."

CHAPTER THIRTY-ONE

HARPER

The next day, Harper sat in the shower, letting the hot water hit her back. She was miserable. Miserable about Bryant. Miserably sick. She held her stomach, so tired of the way this flu was making her feel. She'd made an appointment to go in and get checked out, though she knew it was useless. There was nothing they could do with the flu. Still, for the length of time she'd had it, she was starting to think it was some rare form.

She'd talked to her mother the night before, telling her about her sickness and about her new job, telling her about the town, telling her about everything except Bryant. She wasn't ready yet. She couldn't go there. Every time the conversation took a natural turn in that direction, she directed it elsewhere.

She reached up, turning off the water and remaining still, trying to avoid any sudden movements. After a few moments, she stood, steadying herself before pulling the towel from the rack. Her legs lifted one-by-one over the sides of the bathtub cautiously, as the towel warmed her shivering body. She felt weak—both from lack of food and lack of sleep. Approaching the mirror, she couldn't deny the fact that her eyes were practically lifeless, her skin sallow.

It had been nearly three weeks since she'd been able to keep a meal down, just over two weeks since she found out about her husband, and one week since she'd been able to force herself to suffer through a day at work. It was ridiculous the amount of hours she was missing, and though the hospital had been extremely reasonable with her, they needed to see a doctor's note at this point, and she couldn't blame them. So, she'd finally given in and made the appointment. She hoped and prayed that they could remedy this somehow. A girl could only take so much ginger ale and saltines.

Once she had pulled on her sweatpants and a baggy T-shirt, she descended the stairs, walking toward the front door slowly. With her purse on her arm and her cell phone placed in the inside pocket, she reached for her keys, pulling them off the hook and easing out the door. When she closed the door, it was with all of her strength, and she jiggled the handle extra for good measure. This routine was a habit she'd picked up since the Myrtle Beach trip. Luckily, there had been no more issues with doors being left open.

She walked down the small sidewalk, pressing the button on her key fob to unlock the car. When she stepped to cross in front of her car, a sudden movement caught her eye. A black and brown snake darted out from behind her tire, shooting across her path. She jumped back, letting out a horrified scream and losing her balance as she fell to the ground.

SNAP. She heard the sound as she hit the pavement, felt the pain radiating up the wrist she'd landed on.

"Oh god," she cried out, too tired and nauseous to move.

She looked around, watching for the snake. She hadn't seen exactly where it had gone. As she finally tried to sit up, another pain shot through her wrist. She bit her lip, fat tears suddenly filling her eyes. She lay back on the ground, letting self-pity finally find her. What on earth was she going to do? Not just about this moment, but about her entire life? It wasn't supposed to go this way. None of it. And now that it had, she wasn't sure what to do to fix it. Or if she even wanted to.

Just then, she heard a door slam. She looked up to see Jason rushing toward her, throwing a T-shirt on over his head. She didn't have time to appreciate his chiseled chest as he lowered himself down beside her.

"Oh my god, Harper, are you okay? Are you hurt?" His hands hovered above her, afraid to touch her.

She shook her head, feeling embarrassed. "I think I broke my wrist."

"What? Here, let me look at it," he said, holding his hand out. She placed the throbbing wrist in his hand cautiously, noticing the already-swollen lump.

"Oooh," he said, inhaling sharply. "Yeah, that looks bad. We need to get you to the hospital. Where are your keys?"

She pointed to her bag where it had fallen from her grasp. "I'm okay, honestly. It just hurts."

"You can't drive yourself. Not like that. Here, come on," he placed a hand around her waist, "let me help you up." He lifted her easily, practically carrying her to the passenger's seat and helping her to buckle in. He was insanely close to her, and she noticed for the first time, that he smelled like fresh soap and his hair was slightly wet. He must've just finished showering.

He rushed to the driver's side and pulled out of the driveway quickly. "Hold on, okay?" he told her, looking directly into her eyes before he turned off their road. "Everything's going to be okay."

She leaned her head back on the seat, swallowing. He had no idea how badly she hoped that were true.

CHAPTER THIRTY-TWO

HARPER

Harper lay in the hospital bed, the pain still radiating through her at lightning speed. It was ridiculous how painful it was. She'd never broken anything, but with the ever-growing amount of purple surrounding her swelling, she was almost positive that was what had happened. Finally, she saw a familiar face approaching her.

"Uh-oh, what happened?" Doctor Andrews asked as he approached her.

"I fell," she said, holding up her wrist. "And I heard a snap."

The doctor winced. "Yeah, that doesn't look good. We'll take you up to X-Ray and see about getting it confirmed. You know, if you didn't want to come to work, you could've just told us," he joked, looking over at Jason who was waiting patiently in the chair beside her. "This must be your husband. It's nice to finally meet you."

Harper felt as red as Jason grew. "Oh, no!" They both attempted to correct the doctor at the same time.

Jason laughed, conceding to let Harper finish. "Sorry, no.

This isn't my husband. Jason's my neighbor. He saw me fall and drove me here."

"Oh. Well, nice to meet you, anyway," the doctor said, typing something into the iPad in his hands. "I'll get a nurse to take you down to X-Ray shortly, okay? Sit tight."

Harper nodded. After a few moments, a nurse appeared. Jason agreed to wait by her bed while Harper was taken down the hall. Once they were away from him, a nurse that Harper didn't recognize asked, "Okay, so I do have to ask... there's no chance you could be pregnant, is there?"

Harper shook her head, but froze. "I have PCOS, so my cycles are irregular. I've been told it will likely be hard for me to conceive, so probably not."

The nurse nodded, a look of genuine concern on her face. "Okay," she said patiently, "well, let's take a test just to be on the safe side, and then we'll get you in."

Harper agreed, taking a cup as the nurse grabbed one from the wall and handed it to her. She walked into the bathroom, her hands shaking. There was *no* way she was pregnant...her sickness had only been the flu, right?

CHAPTER THIRTY-THREE

BRYANT

Bryant sat in class, staring at the heads of all of his students as they took a pop quiz. Tests and quizzes were the only quiet moments he was allowed in a day, and so he had been taking advantage of that as much as possible. He needed the quiet. He needed time to think.

He checked his phone again. He was used to updates from her throughout the day, but they'd abruptly stopped after his accidental confession. What an idiot he'd been. If he hadn't confessed, there's a good chance none of this would've ever come out. If he hadn't done it in the first place, it definitely wouldn't have come out.

When the bell rang a few minutes later, he patted his desk. "That's the bell. Everyone hand in your quizzes as you leave. See you guys tomorrow."

The teenagers stood from their desks, beginning with their usual chatter as they slid their papers into the tray he had waiting for them.

He locked his drawers, closing his computer and grabbing his phone from his desk as he headed out of his classroom and locked the door.

On his way home, he dialed her number, waiting to hear her voice. He eventually did, but in the form of her voicemail message.

"Hey," he said, "just wanted to say I'm thinking about you. I, um, I miss you. A lot. I'm thinking about you...about us, all the time. I hope you're feeling better. I'll see you soon."

He closed his phone, praying she would call him back. He had to win her back. He had to earn her trust again. Without Harper, he was nothing.

WHEN BRYANT WALKED in the house, he was surprised by the quiet. Harper had told him she was calling in that morning, so he was sure she would still be home. He glanced at the empty lock screen of his phone once again. Where could she be?

He glanced out the window, looking at his sole car in the driveway, and began dialing her number again.

This time, she picked up.

"Hello?"

"Harper, where are you?"

"I'm pulling in now," she said. "I'll be in, in just a second." He felt relief wash over him at her words, sliding the phone into his pocket as he heard the call end.

"I love you, too," he whispered, long after she was gone from the line.

CHAPTER THIRTY-FOUR

HARPER

Harper and Jason climbed from the car in front of her house. She wanted to tell him thank you for helping her and for not asking questions when she'd returned from her X-ray with tears in her eyes, but she was having trouble forming words. He seemed to understand, putting an arm around her shoulders and pulling her in for a hug.

"It's going to be okay," he promised, his warm breath in her hair.

"You don't know that."

He nodded, his chin resting on her scalp. "I do. Eventually, it's going to work out." Without waiting for permission, he pressed his lips into her forehead. "Call me if you need anything," he whispered. "Please take care of yourself, Harper." As he began walking away from her and up his driveway, he called over his shoulder, "I mean it."

Harper stood still, feeling the impression of his lips on her skin as she watched him walk away. Her feelings were all over the place; she was a complete mess. How on earth was she going to deal with all the news the doctor's office had given her? How was she going to deal with her failing marriage now that a baby—a baby she'd thought she couldn't have—was thrown into the mix?

She walked up the cement walkway in a trance, headed for the front door. Bryant opened it quickly. "Oh my god, what happened?" he asked, staring at her cast.

She stepped past him and into the house. "I fell," she said simply. "On my way to the doctor."

"And it's broken?" he asked, reaching for it.

She kept it away from him. "Yes, it's broken."

"Are you...I mean, are you okay?" he asked. "Why didn't you call me?"

"I'm fine," she said. "I just...I didn't think about it."

"You didn't think about it?" he demanded, obviously upset.

"I had other things on my mind, Bryant. I was in pain. I was sick. My first thought wasn't to call you—"

"You've always called me when you were hurt or sick or—"

"We aren't who we were then!" she shrieked. "Everything we do now...every decision we make, it's all different. We have to handle it differently."

"What does that mean?" He tilted his head to the side.

"I don't know," she said, pressing her fingers to the bridge of her nose.

"I love you, Harper..."

"I know."

"You know?" he asked. "You don't love me, too?"

"Of course I love you, Bryant. That doesn't just go away."

"Then we can fix this, right? We have to fix this."

"I don't know." She stepped back as he moved toward her. "I want to go take a bath. I feel disgusting."

"Okay," he said, his face falling slightly. "Let me help you."

"No," she said too quickly, holding out a hand to keep him

from moving any closer. "I've got it." Without waiting for a response, she turned away, headed up the stairs.

"What did the doctor say?" he asked. "Do you have the flu?"

She closed her eyes, not turning back around to face him from the stairs. She hadn't made the decision to lie until right at that moment. It was instinct. She had to protect herself, and giving away that secret made her vulnerable. "Yes," she said coolly, continuing up the stairs. "Just the flu."

CHAPTER THIRTY-FIVE

HARPER

Two days later, Harper set out for her first day back at work. The medicine the doctor had prescribed for morning sickness had worked wonders, and she was finally back to feeling somewhat normal again.

She held a cup of coffee in one hand—decaf—and her keys in the other. Bryant had already left for the day, seemingly over his fear of disturbing her as she got ready. As she climbed into the car, her phone began ringing, causing her to jump. It was a number she didn't recognize. She maneuvered her purse over her cast carefully, using her unbroken wrist to lift the phone to her ear.

"Hello?"

"Hello, may I speak to Harper Page, please?"

"Speaking," she said, not recognizing the cool voice on the other end of the line.

"Mrs. Page, this is Cara from The Women's Center. I'm calling to confirm your appointment for two o'clock today."

"I'm sorry, my what?" she asked, wrinkling her brow in confusion. She turned the knob, lowering the volume on the radio, though she knew that wasn't the issue.

The woman cleared her throat. "Um, your appointment. We have you down for two o'clock, is that not correct?"

Harper shook her head. "I don't understand. What is the appointment for? I never made any appointment."

The woman hummed, clicking her tongue. "Well, perhaps there's been a mistake. You didn't make an appointment with us? You're sure? I can remove you, but it may be a while before we can get you in again."

"I didn't make any appointment," she confirmed. "There has to be a mistake."

"Okay," the woman said, sounding like she didn't totally believe her. "Well, I'm sorry to have bothered you. I will get that cancelled right now."

"Thank you," Harper said, hanging up the phone and feeling frazzled. She sat in the driveway, staring into space as she tried to figure out what had just happened. *The Women's Center*—that was what the receptionist had called it, right? What was that?

She Googled the name, finding a few results before she located one in Shallotte. She clicked on the website, scrolling through a pink layout. The four options on her screen were: **STDs, Abortion, Birth Control, and Emergency Contraceptive.** Below that, she could enter a zip code to find a local branch. She bit her bottom lip as she read over the list again.

Was this some sort of sick joke? Why would that number have called her? Why would she have an appointment with them? She closed her eyes. The only person who knew about the pregnancy was her doctor. But why would he make an appointment without even contacting her? She took a deep, haggard breath. Maybe she was being dramatic. Perhaps the center dealt with pregnancy and he had scheduled her a prenatal appointment. Had he mentioned that? Honestly, her brain was so fuzzy with memories of that moment, she couldn't remember. That had to be it. How else would they have her phone number or know about her condition? If she could catch him today at work, she would be sure to ask him.

Placing her phone back into her bag, she turned up the radio once again and drove away, trying desperately to calm her racing mind.

CHAPTER THIRTY-SIX

HARPER

On her lunch break, Harper roamed the halls of the hospital, waiting outside the room where Doctor Andrews was seeing a patient. When he walked out, she nearly jumped up as she rushed toward him.

"Oh, hey, Harper, what's up? How's your wrist feeling?" he asked.

She glanced at it as if it were an afterthought. "Oh, fine. It's fine. Listen, can I talk to you?" she asked.

"Of course," he said, pointing to the empty room next to them. "In here?"

She nodded, following his lead into the small room and sitting on the exam table out of instinct.

"Is everything all right?" he asked as he shut the door, laying the chart in his hands down on the counter so his attention was solely on her.

"I'm fine," she said, touching her stomach. "I just...I got a weird call this morning."

He cocked his head to the side. "Okay..."

"From The Women's Center?"

"Oh," he said, nodding seriously. "Are you considering

having an abortion?" He asked it with no judgement, though she instantly felt judged.

"No, of course not. I…I mean, this baby…I just wasn't expecting the phone call, is all. I didn't know if maybe you'd called them for me."

His eyes went wide and he cracked a small smile as if he thought she were joking. When she didn't smile back, his faded. "Harper, I would never. You know we couldn't do that. Now, of course, if you asked us to set you up with someone— here or otherwise—we would be happy to. But I would never do that without your consent."

"I guess I knew that, I just don't understand how they could've gotten my number." She crossed her arms as a cold chill ran over her. "It's strange timing, that's all."

He nodded. "Is it possible your husband called them? How is he handling the news?"

She frowned. "I haven't told him yet."

"Why do you think that is?" he asked, crossing one leg over the other and leaning forward.

"I'm just…waiting for the right time."

The doctor pressed his lips into a thin line. "Are you sure you wouldn't like to talk to someone? There's no pressure, but Doctor Ambrose is excellent. It's completely covered since you're an employee. There's really no downside, and she can help you work through everything."

She smiled sadly. "Thanks, really. I'm okay, though." She stood from the exam table. "Thanks for answering my question."

"Of course," he said, standing as well and pulling open the door. "Good luck, Harper."

WHEN HARPER GOT BACK to her desk, Devon had a funny look on his face. The rest of her coworkers had been strangely cold to her since she had returned to work as well, and she definitely felt like more of an outsider than she had in a long time.

"Everything okay?" she asked, sliding into her seat and tossing her cup in the trash.

Devon nodded, not bothering to say much. Savannah mumbled something under her breath that made Collette laugh. Harper signed onto her computer, trying to ignore them. She felt as though she were in high school again, with the same catty girls that caused her to eat lunch alone in the bathroom stall, pretending she would rather be alone than with anyone else.

Truth was, Harper didn't like to be alone. She never had. Growing up in a big family, being alone felt strange. She wasn't entirely comfortable unless she was surrounded by others.

When she opened her computer, there was an email from the head of Human Resources, asking her to step into her office when she had the chance.

Harper slid her chair out from under the desk, standing up. No one would meet her eye. She tried to smile at the coworkers who had once been friends, tried to get some reassurance from anywhere at that moment, but they weren't offering.

She walked quietly toward the end of the hall, where the office was. Janine Fremont was a short, plump woman in her mid-fifties with kind eyes and graying red hair that sat atop her head in the same style every day. She wore bright pink lipstick that always ended up on her coffee-stained teeth.

Harper had seen her a few times, but only spoken to her on the day she was hired. So, as she walked into her office, knocking on the open door, she tried desperately to read the expression on her unfamiliar face.

"Hello," she said, "you wanted to see me?"

"I did," Janine said politely, standing up and holding out a hand to gesture for her to sit down. "Come on in." Harper sat. "Now, Harper, when you arrived, you were made aware of the hospital's sick and vacation time policies, correct?"

"I was," Harper said, swallowing. "I can get a doctor's excuse as to why I was out for so long."

Janine held her hand up to stop her. "You were also made aware that we monitor employees' social media accounts, correct?"

"Of course."

She frowned, turning the computer around for her to see what was on her screen. It was a photo of Harper laying on the beach, her red bathing suit against her pale skin. She gasped as she realized it was taken not so long ago when they'd gone to Myrtle Beach. She hadn't realized anyone had been taking her picture. Upon further inspection, she noticed the picture was from a Facebook post with the caption "**Living my best life. This trip has been all I needed and more! #FunNSun**"

Looking even closer, she gasped as she saw the picture had been posted just three days ago, from her own account. "I didn't post that. I've been sick all week. I swear to you I have."

Janine folded her hands across her desk. "Even so, it'd be hard to prove. Your coworkers are all, understandably, upset. Several of them had to work extra to cover your shifts over the past few weeks. To find out that you lied to us, to them, well...I'm sure you understand why we'll have to let you go. We have a zero tolerance policy with this sort of thing, especially since you're so new." Her eyes were soft, yet her voice was firm. "I'll have to ask you to clean out your locker today and go home."

She shook her head, tears welling in her eyes. "I don't...I don't understand. I was here just two days ago in the hospital. I have horrible morning sickness. Doctor Andrews can vouch for me."

"Two days ago?"

"Yes," she insisted.

"What about the week before that? Unless Doctor Andrews can verify that you were home sick for the week before, I'm afraid there's nothing we can do."

"I could sue you..." she threatened, feeling herself get worked up. "I'm pregnant."

The woman's eyes wavered a bit, and she stood up. "I'm afraid you'll have to get into contact with our legal team for anything further on this matter." She held her arm out toward the door. "You may clean out your locker now."

Harper stood, feeling as though she were going to be sick. She couldn't be sure if it was the baby or the situation causing it. She glanced down, pulling her phone from her pocket and clicking on the blue Facebook app. She waited as the dots spun, and then gasped when the screen changed.

What the hell?

She stared down at the gray screen, red letters warning her that something was very, very wrong.

Sorry! You've used an old password. Please try logging in with your new password.

CHAPTER THIRTY-SEVEN

BRYANT

Bryant watched anxiously as Harper walked through the front door. It was embarrassing to admit that he'd be waiting for her so impatiently. Since his confession, each time she was away from him, he grew incredibly worried that she may never come back.

She set her bag down, hanging up her keys and brushing the hairs that had come loose from her bun out of her face.

"Hey, babe," he said, watching her as she made her way across the room. "How was work?"

"I don't know," she answered honestly, sinking into the couch next to him. "I...Bryant, I got fired today."

The words slammed into his chest, causing him to do a double take. "You what?"

"I got fired," she repeated. "I've just been driving around, trying to make sense of it all. I don't understand. Someone hacked my Facebook and posted this picture of me at the beach. They made it seem like we'd been there this week—like that was why I'd been missing work. Everyone's furious. I can't even access my Facebook to take the photo down. Not to mention that I don't even know how they *got* the picture.

It's like someone was following us, Bryant. My password's been changed. I'm really trying not to freak out here, but I don't know what's going on."

"What are you talking about? What picture? They just fired you without a warning? How could they do that? How would someone have hacked your account? You didn't click on any weird links did you?"

"No! Of course not," she said angrily, tears in her eyes. "I don't understand how any of it could've happened. I just...we really needed me to have that job. The next nearest hospital is an hour away, at least."

He reached for her, surprised when she fell into his arms without a struggle. He rubbed her hair, rocking back and forth and trying to pretend he wasn't freaked out. "Okay, well don't panic. There'll be some sort of explanation. Photoshop or something. Hacking does happen. It's okay. It's all going to be okay. We'll figure it out. It's not the end of the world."

"No, you don't understand," she said, her eyes closing as she pulled away from him.

"What don't I understand?"

She looked down, her fingers running across the fabric on her shirt. "Bryant, I'm pregnant."

He swallowed. Blinked. Opened his mouth. Closed his mouth. Coughed. *What? What the what?* "You're..."

"Pregnant," she repeated. He knew he had to be wearing a dumbfounded expression, his entire world flipped on its side at the moment. How could that be possible? All this time he'd been worried about Tori being pregnant, and Harper was the one to end up that way. Was he happy? He couldn't tell. Was she?

"How..." *Words. You just need words. Any words will do. Something. Anything.* "How long have you known?"

"Since I went to the doctor for my wrist."

"But you said—"

"I wasn't ready to talk about it." She shook her head. "I don't know what it means for us. I still don't. I don't know where we stand anymore. This baby doesn't change what you did."

"I know that."

"But I do love you," she said firmly, squeezing his hand.

He pulled her hand to his mouth, kissing her fingers. "I love you so much, Harper. I love this baby. I just want us to go back to the way we were."

She blinked back sudden tears. "I don't know if that's possible…"

He inhaled sharply, his eyes begging her to reconsider. He could still see the old them. He could remember the way he could make her laugh without trying. He remembered the nights he spent painting her toenails when she'd pinched a nerve in her shoulder and couldn't stand to move it. He could picture them dancing in the kitchen their first night in their Chicago apartment. He remembered asking her dad for her hand in marriage. He remembered the man Harper made him, and the woman he loved more than anything in the world. He'd been blinded momentarily, but that didn't take away from what he felt for her. "Please don't say that."

"I don't, Bryant. I'm sorry. But that doesn't mean I don't want to give us a chance. For the baby."

His heart leapt. "Really?"

She nodded, not meeting his eye. "I need to learn to trust you again. Trust has never come easy to me, and you've," she sucked in a breath, "you've really hurt me. But I do love you. I want this baby to know how good we used to be, you know?"

He leaned in, ready to scoop her up and give her every piece of him again, but she stopped him, leaning back. "I'm…not ready for…that. I just can't." She shook her head.

He nodded, feeling a bit slighted. "Okay. Just…just let me know what you need, Harper. Anything."

"I just…I need time. Space. A bit of air. I need to get my head together and figure out exactly what I want here. What I want from you. From us. From all of it. I need to figure everything out."

"What can I do?"

"Just be patient with me," she said. "I want to get back to who we were, but I need to figure out who I am again."

"What does that mean…exactly?"

She closed her eyes, running a finger across her bottom lip. "I've been giving this a lot of thought. I think I want to go back to Chicago for a bit. I miss it. I think being home would give me some clarity."

"But…this is your home now. That's what you said. Your home is wherever I am."

"I know I said that, but this is…it's just something I need to do. For me."

"Okay, when? I'll let the school know."

She placed a hand on his chest and then she said the words that let him know she was slipping out of his grasp before his very eyes. "No, Bryant. *I* need to go. Alone."

CHAPTER THIRTY-EIGHT

BRYANT

The next morning, Bryant woke up early. He hadn't been able to sleep much the night before, so maybe *woke up* is an exaggeration. He rolled over on the air mattress, surprised to see Harper standing in the doorway.

"Good morning," he said sleepily.

"Good morning," she greeted him. "I didn't mean to wake you. I wanted to see about checking on flights."

He nodded, watching her glide across the room and take a seat at the computer desk. "Of course. Hey, listen, are you sure you don't want me to go with you? It might be good for us to get away for a bit. Kind of like our Myrtle Beach trip. That was good for us, right?"

"The one that got me fired?" she asked, not looking his way.

"Well, that's certainly not my fault," he argued.

She sighed, smoothing out her forehead wrinkles with her palm. "I know it isn't. I just...I really think this is something I need to do alone. I appreciate the offer, though."

"Are you leaving me?" he asked, voicing the fear that had filled his mind, running on repeat for hours now.

She looked at him then, her eyes filled with sorrow. "Is that what you want?"

"Of course not," he insisted, scooting toward the end of the mattress so he could reach for her hand. She didn't extend it, but she didn't pull away as he took it, either. "All I want is for us to be better. All I want…is you, Harper. Just you. Us. Our baby. Our family. I want it all with you."

She squeezed his hand when he squeezed hers, and when he leaned in for a kiss, she didn't pull away. Her lips remained closed, a clear boundary drawn, and he respected it. It was better than nothing. It was progress.

"I never thought I could have kids, Bryant. I'm not sure I ever even wanted them, but it was never a possibility, so I didn't worry about figuring that out. I'm…I'm really scared. We aren't ready for this. This wasn't in the plan. I still want my career. We're… shaky at best. Everything's so messed up."

He pulled her onto his lap, breathing in the warm, honey scent he'd missed so much. "Harper, everything's going to be okay. Do you hear me?" He stared into her almond eyes with hope. "I promise you it will. I'm going to take care of you. And our baby. You're going to have the high-powered hospital administration career you've always wanted. You're going to have everything. I promise." She nuzzled into his chest, and for a moment, it felt like his indiscretions might be forgotten. "I love you so much," he whispered, a piece of her hair teasing his lip as he breathed.

"I love you, too," she promised.

He wrapped his arms around her waist, resting one hand on her belly. "How are you feeling? Any more morning sickness?"

"The doctor gave me medicine for it. It seems to be helping."

"Did you…did you get to see it? Did they do an ultrasound?"

She shook her head. "No. It's still too early. But soon."

"Will you let me come?"

She twisted her mouth in thought. "Do you want to?"

"More than anything," he said honestly.

She nodded. "Okay, then. I still have to schedule the appointment. I guess I can do that today...not like I have anything else to do." She sucked in a breath. "Oh, no. *Insurance.* With me out of a job, we don't have insurance." Her eyes filled with worry.

He kissed her fingers. "I'll get us both added onto mine. It may be a few weeks before it'll kick in, but it's going to be okay. I'll do that today."

"Okay," she said. "I'll hold off on an appointment, then. Until we know more."

"Is that safe?" he asked.

"What choice do we have? It's not like we can afford a few thousand dollars in medical bills from one appointment. Especially not with me out of a job."

He swallowed, trying not to let her see his fear. That was the last thing he could worry about at the moment, though he knew they were going to be in trouble if she didn't get back to work soon. His salary would hardly cover their basic bills. "Okay. Well, I'll see what I can find out today. Speaking of," he glanced at his phone on the floor, "I need to go hop in the shower." He kissed her quickly and stood up, helping her back into the chair. "You can join me if you'd like."

She smiled softly, looking at the computer screen. "Thanks, but I need to look at tickets. Mom's going to pay for it, so I need to get the dates and times lined up."

He bit his lip, afraid to say anything else that may cause a fight, and walked out of the room. He darted across the hall, trying not to panic as his wife planned her escape from him. He turned on the water and jumped back as the high pressure stream of the shower nearly hit him.

What the hell?

He walked back out of the room, hurrying toward the office. "Harper?"

"Yeah?" she called, not looking back over her shoulder.

"The shower is messed up again."

"What do you mean messed up?" She stopped typing, turning to look at him finally.

"Someone messed with the shower stream. That's the second time this has happened."

"Someone who?"

"I don't know," he said angrily, starting to feel paranoid. It wasn't like he'd forgotten about the nightgown and subscriptions, but things had been quiet for a while. He was starting to think he was being overanxious. But, not now. Something was definitely wrong. "Are you sure you didn't do it?"

"Of course not. Why would I? I rarely take showers, anyway. You know I prefer baths."

He shrugged. "Well, what else could it be? Someone's breaking in here."

"Breaking in?" She let out a sudden laugh. "And what? Changing our shower head? That's it? C'mon, you don't honestly believe that."

"Why don't you? It's not like it's the only strange thing going on around here. Slashed tires, the lingerie, the magazines."

She ran a finger over her lip. "I don't know, Bryant. It just seems a little crazy, that's all."

He shook his head. "Watch out."

"What?"

He moved toward her. "Let me see the computer for just a second."

"Why?" she asked.

"I want to look up who lived in this house before us."

She wiggled her fingers in the air, standing up obligingly.

"What—do you actually think there's a ghost haunting us?" She giggled, obviously trying to seem more calm than she felt.

"I don't know what to think, Harper, but I'm going to find out the truth about what's going on around here."

She didn't laugh any more as he typed, instead, she watched him search—trying desperately to find something, anything, that might explain the strange things that had befallen them since they'd moved to Lancaster Mills. Even more so since they'd met their neighbors.

CHAPTER THIRTY-NINE

HARPER

Bryant searched through the papers from their mortgage closing, finding the name of their seller and tracking her down on Facebook. He sent her a message, asking if there was a way they could get in touch. He said he needed some information about the house, and then once he got ahold of her, he told Harper he would ask her all about the strange things that were happening and the even stranger couple next door.

After he left for work, promising to let her know the second he heard *anything,* Harper sat in front of the computer, staring at a screen and wondering what to do next. Going to Chicago was still important to her. She still felt like it was the right thing to do...but could she leave now? When Bryant was so...*afraid?* It no longer felt like an option.

She glanced out the window, surprised to see Jason and Tori below in their yard. She rolled closer to the glass, trying to make out what was happening. It looked like an argument, though they'd always seemed so perfect. What on earth could they be fighting about?

Then it hit her, like it so often did, the remembering. What her husband had done. There were fleeting moments when the truth seemed to slip her mind, but it always came back. It wouldn't leave her for long. The couple spoke heatedly, Tori's arms waving wildly at her sides. Harper leaned even closer toward the pane, but she still couldn't make out what they were saying. Could she open the window without them noticing?

She watched for a few more moments before curiosity got the best of her and she unlatched the window, easing it up carefully. No sooner had she slid it up an inch than her worst nightmare occurred. Suddenly, the watcher became the watched. Jason and Tori's eyes darted toward her as the window groaned, and she knew she'd been caught. She closed it quickly, her heart pounding, and darted away from the window. Her breathing was erratic as she tried to reason with herself that they may not assume she had been trying to eavesdrop. Perhaps she'd just been opening the window in order to let in a breeze and then closed it when she realized she'd interrupted a quiet moment. Yes, that was it. That would be her story.

The sudden ringing of the doorbell interrupted her thoughts. She paced the office, trying to decide what she should do, hoping they would just go away. When the doorbell rang again, she opened the office door and hurried down the stairs, her pulse so loud she could hear nothing else. She whipped open the door, trying to catch her breath, and stared at Jason.

"Hey, sorry—" she blurted out. *So much for playing it cool.* "I wasn't eavesdropping. I just…I needed some fresh air, and when I saw you guys were outside I—"

"It's fine, Harper, that's not why I'm here."

"Oh," she said, her jaw dropping. "It's not?"

"No," he said, shaking his head. "No, it's not. Is Bryant here?"

"Oh," she said again, her tone giving her away.

His expression changed, and he stepped into the house without permission. "You knew?" he asked, and suddenly she knew *he knew.*

She nodded. "I'm sorry...I should've told you. I'm just... I'm still processing."

"Yeah," he said, "me too. What are you...what are you doing?"

"I don't know," she said honestly. "I'm thinking of going back to Chicago for a while."

"Don't—" he said, stepping forward and taking her hand. "You can't leave."

She stared at him, her brow furrowed. "Why not?"

"Because...well..." He leaned down, catching her by surprise as his lips connected with hers. For a moment, she was still, feeling the unfamiliar skin against hers and the kiss that felt so new. He put a hand to her cheek, cupping her face. He smelled different—warmer than Bryant somehow. *Bryant.*

She stepped back, shaking her head. "I can't. I'm sorry...I —you should go." She rubbed her bottom lip, wiping away his taste. Coffee and cinnamon.

"I'm sorry, I don't know what I was thinking. I've wanted to do that for so—"

"You're married," she said firmly, putting a hand to his chest to stop him as he tried to move closer. "*I'm* married. I just...I can't do this. I can't—" She broke off into sudden tears, one hand over her mouth. "You need to go," she said with a sob.

He took a step back, his eyes locked with hers. "I'm so sorry, Harper. I never meant to upset you. I...I care about you. I wanted you to know that."

She nodded. "Thank you." It was all she could manage to say.

"If you...um, if you need anything, I'm here." He pulled the door open, disappearing out of it quickly without another word.

When she was sure he could no longer hear her, she sank into a nearby chair, one hand over her mouth, trying desperately to stifle the sobs that tore out of her. What had she done? What had Bryant done? What could they do now? The pain of everything that had happened crashed into her like ocean waves, tears flooding her eyes as she finally gave in to the overwhelming sense of grief for what had been. What may never be again.

She put her hand to her stomach, to the child whose life would be affected by her every move, and cried louder, because what on earth was she going to do?

CHAPTER FORTY

HARPER

Bryant arrived home three hours early, finding Harper still on the couch, where she had remained since Jason's departure. Finally, her tears had dried, though she still felt as hopeless and alone as ever.

"What are you doing home early?" she asked, though she could tell by the look on his face that something was very wrong.

"I got a message back from the old owner."

Harper shot up from the couch. "What did she say?"

He swallowed, unlocking his phone. His hands were shaking. "It's not good, Harp. It's...I think we may be in danger."

"Danger?" she asked. "What on earth are you talking about?"

"She wouldn't tell me much," he said, "but she said that she had strange encounters with them. She said that she always felt like they were watching her."

"What?"

"Yeah," he confirmed. "She gave me her email, and I asked her to tell me more about the neighbors. I asked if they ever bothered her. And I mean, she didn't mention the shower thing, but she said they gave her the creeps. I asked her to tell me more, but she hasn't responded. I'm...I'm really freaking out here, Harper." His nervous laugh and the way he ran his hand over the back of his neck told her that was true. This was not okay.

"We need to leave," she said firmly. "We need to go back to Chicago."

He swallowed. "But what about work? And insurance? And our house?"

"We'll figure something out. What I care about right now is our safety. The baby's safety. I can't...I can't stay here." She paused, debating on telling him about the kiss, but decided against it. It didn't matter. They were leaving. They were going to get away.

"Okay," he said seriously. "I'll contact a realtor tomorrow." He reached for her arm, running a thumb over it. "It's all going to be okay."

She pressed her lips together, fighting the urge to pull away from him. She wanted to be angry—and she was. But she couldn't deny that they were in this together. That they would need each other to make it through everything that lay ahead. She had no idea what the future held, but she couldn't do it alone, and as her husband leaned forward, rocking her in his arms, she was immensely thankful she wouldn't have to.

CHAPTER FORTY-ONE

HARPER

Two weeks later, Harper sat at the computer, staring at the blank screen. She was supposed to be packing, but the days where she could go nonstop were long since over. With the baby growing, her symptoms—namely exhaustion—were getting worse every day.

So, she'd taken to searching for a new apartment for them in Chicago, and gawking at the price increase in the few months since they'd been gone. She didn't even want to think about daycares, which as they currently stood were a whopping thousand dollars a month. But it was home. They'd make it work. They had to. What was really stalling them was searching for new jobs in Chicago. The idea of losing insurance with a baby on the way was debilitating. Not to mention trying to cram into her parents' home for too long, which had never been appealing. They needed their own space.

Overwhelmed with her search, she'd found a new topic to begin researching. She scrolled through pages and pages of 'Tori and Jason Fuller' results.

Finally, she saw something that caught her eye: a headline from fourteen years ago.

Eleven Dead, Two Survive Dublin House Fire

She clicked on the link, skimming through the article.

Eleven people are dead after a house fire in Dublin early Monday morning. Around 4:00 A.M., police and fire departments were called to a residence on East Filmore Street in Dublin. Upon arrival, firemen were able to rescue two victims from the residence. Shortly after, the home collapsed, killing the remaining inhabitants— Marshall and Evelyn Fuller and their nine children. Six of the children were placed in the Fullers' care through the foster care system. The sole survivors were Jason Fuller, 18, and Tori Breeland, 16.

At this time, residents are being asked to stay away from this side of town. Streets are blocked off and fire crews are working hard to clean up the mess left behind by this devastation. We are being told that police do not suspect foul play, but they are conducting a thorough investigation. The report will be released later this month.

She scrolled down a bit to a brightly lit shot of Jason and Tori standing in front of a smoldering building. The night was dark around them, and it looked as if the flash had caught them off guard, making their already pale faces even more ashen. They had thick, gray blankets around their shoulders, and Jason had an arm around her. Even then, he was protective over her.

Harper couldn't help but feel like it was strange that Tori and Jason had been foster siblings—it seemed like a gray area for relationships at best—but she pushed the thought aside as she backed out of the article.

She scrolled back up to the top, searching for their names along with a new location: Dublin, Tennessee. The top article was one about a homeschooling group led by Marshall and Evelyn Fuller. She clicked on it, scrolling through it without reading the quotes from Evelyn about how wholesome their life had become since they'd made the decision to home-school their children, foster care children excluded. They were leading a group from the community on weekly field trips and seeking out fellow homeschooling parents to join them.

Harper couldn't deny the chill that ran down her spine as she stared at the picture at the top of the article, where Marshall and Evelyn, clad in bland suits with their hair perfectly coiffed, smiled up at the camera. They were almost too perfect. Evelyn with her red-brown hair and large teeth, and Marshall with his strawberry-blond hair and circular glasses. They were practically an ad for cheesy studio shots the nineties had made popular.

She scrolled down, noticing another picture of the Fullers with their three children: Jason, Jessica, and Jordyn. The siblings had their wiry arms wrapped around each other, the girls in long skirts and polo shirts and Jason in khakis and a blue shirt and tie.

As Harper looked even closer, she let out a gasp, covering her mouth with one hand as she felt sickness climbing into her throat. She read over the caption just to be sure. **Marshall and Evelyn Fuller pictured with their three children: (left to right) Jessica, Jordyn, and Jason.** She sucked in a deep breath.

The man she was staring at was not Jason Fuller.

CHAPTER FORTY-TWO

HARPER

Harper printed the page quickly, watching over her shoulder as panic set in. She exited out of the website, pushing the chair up to the desk as she dialed Bryant's number.

"Hello?" he asked.

"C-come home," she said, her voice shaking. "Please come home."

"Harper? What is it? What's wrong? Are you okay?"

"I'm okay…I just need you to come home. I…I found something."

"What did you find?" he demanded. "You're scaring me."

"I just…please come—" She squealed as she heard the doorbell sounding below, and she knew who it must be.

"What is it?" he asked.

"Someone's at the door," she whispered. "Someone's here."

"Who is it?"

"I don't know." She sank to the floor. "Jason and Tori… they aren't who we think they are, Bryant."

"What are you talking about?"

"I think we're in very real danger here. Please just come home."

"Listen to me," he said firmly, the fear evident in his voice. She heard his class quiet down in the background, and she knew they must sense that something was wrong as well. "Get in a closet. The baseball bat is in the back of ours. Get in there and *do not* come out until I get home, okay? I'm leaving now." She heard him shutting a door that told her he truly was. "I love you, okay?"

"I love you, too," she said softly, listening carefully as the doorbell down below rang again.

She stood up, walking toward the door and creeping across the hall while trying to make as little noise as possible. She couldn't let them hear her, though she knew they knew she was home. Her car was in the driveway, after all. Her throat was dry as she sank into the closet, taking hold of the metal baseball bat and promising the child in her stomach that she'd protect him or her with everything she had.

After a moment, the doorbell stopped ringing and she listened to her own shallow breathing. Had they given up? Were they gone? What did they want with her?

She jumped, letting out a scream as a piercing noise rang out. Her phone. She reached in her pocket, staring at a number she vaguely recognized on her screen.

"Hello?"

"Hello? Is this Ms. Page?"

"It is, who is this?"

"This is Angie calling from The Women's Center. I was just calling to follow up about the form you filled out on our website. I wanted to see if now was a good time to chat?"

"A form on your website? What are you talking about?"

"You didn't fill out a form on our website?" she asked skeptically.

"Of course I didn't. I've never even heard of you before."

"Ms. Page…it's perfectly okay to be scared, but please don't put off the conversation if you truly do want to know your options. Trust me, there is no judgement here. We help women make the best decision for themselves, and we have trained staff who can answer any and all questions you may have. Then, when the time is right, if you decide to go through with an abortion or adoption, we can guide you through the steps."

"Excuse me?" She reeled back, forgetting that she was trying to be quiet. "An abortion? I would *never.*"

"I understand if you've changed your mind, but our office is a safe space to talk about whatever may be going on in your mind or your life—"

"I haven't *changed my mind,*" she said angrily, "because that was never an option to begin with. Now, I'm not sure if this is some sort of prank, but this is the second time your office has called me."

"I'm sorry, it sounds like I've upset you. I can assure you that this isn't a prank. We are responding to an online query to this number."

"Maybe you misdialed."

"Are you Harper Page?"

"I am." The lady was quiet for a moment. "Look, could you just put me on a do-not-call list?" Harper asked, clutching her stomach.

"I'll…I'll make a note. I'm sorry to have disturbed you, but if something does come up…please know you may call back at any time."

She nodded, though the receptionist couldn't see her. "Thank you. I'm sorry, I don't mean to yell at you."

"I know," she said patiently. "It's a stressful time. Take care, Ms. Page."

With that, Harper pressed the button on her screen to end the call and let out a breath. She sat still, her thoughts racing as she replayed the conversation, listening carefully for the sound of footsteps. Had the person at the door left? The bell hadn't rung in the time that she'd been on the phone. She looked down at her phone as it began to ring again and her screen was lit up with the same number.

"H-hello?"

"Hi! Is this Harper Page?"

"Who is this?" she demanded.

"This is Gracie calling from The Women's Center—"

"Don't call me again!" she screamed, ending the call with shaking fingers. She opened up her recent calls, selecting the number and blocking it. There was no longer any possibility that it was a coincidence that they were calling her. Just like the mail that they hadn't subscribed to continuing to come. Someone was trying to drive them crazy, and it was working.

After a few minutes, she heard Bryant's voice, and relief flooded her. She was safe now. She could breathe easily again.

"Harp?" she heard him calling, and she stood, reaching to open the closet door.

"I'm up here," she said. "In the bedroom. I'm okay."

She heard his hurried footsteps rushing toward her, and as the bedroom door was flung open, he grabbed her, pulling her into a quick hug and kissing her head over and over. One hand went to her stomach. She could feel his heart pounding against her hands. "You're okay? You're sure?" he asked, looking to her belly and then kissing her face again. He cupped her cheeks. "I've never been so worried in my life. I think I broke every speed limit in town on the way here. Are you sure you're okay? What happened?"

She closed her eyes as she offered a soft nod. "I'm okay. Honestly. Whoever was at the door is gone."

"They didn't find you?"

"Find me?" she asked, furrowing her brow. "What do you mean?"

"The...front door was...open," he said, studying her face. "I assumed...oh my god, I was so terrified."

"Wait," she said pushing him away, "what do you mean the front door was open?"

"When I came home, it was standing open."

"Like someone broke in?"

He shrugged. "I don't know, it was just open. Like before. It doesn't look broken into."

"What does that mean?" she asked. "How else could it have been open? Are they in the house?"

That seemed not to have occurred to him as a possibility until that moment. He pressed a finger to his lips and whispered, "Shhh..." as he held her hand and led her from the room. One room at a time, they searched cautiously, trying to find out if they had an unwelcome intruder. As they tiptoed through each room, Harper's heart thudded loudly in her chest, her body ice cold with adrenaline. What was the plan if he did happen to find someone? What would they do?

Luckily, by the end of their search, no such intruder showed up, leaving them with only one conclusion. "Whoever was here," Bryant said as they reached the living room, "is gone now."

"But they got in here somehow," Harper said. It wasn't a question, but Bryant's expression gave her an answer. "I want to change the locks," she said. "It could be whoever took your key before. The mugger."

He didn't seem to agree, but he nodded anyway. "That seems far fetched, but it couldn't hurt to change the locks."

"If not the kids, then who? I mean, do you think it's... could it be Tori and Jason?"

Bryant bit his lip. "I don't know," he whispered, as if the neighbors could be listening to their conversation. For all she knew, they were. "I really don't." He squeezed her hand. "But it's going to be okay. We'll get the locks changed and the house up for sale. As soon as possible, we'll be out of here."

She nodded.

"Harp, what was it you wanted to tell me?"

"What?" she asked, her mind elsewhere.

"When you called, you said there was something I needed to see." He brushed a piece of hair from her eyes, his face full of worry.

"Oh, right," she said, thinking of the paper that lay upstairs. "I, um, I have something to show you." She held his hand, leading him up the stairs cautiously. "I was doing some research earlier. Trying to find out more about Tori and Jason. And...well, I don't really know how to say this."

"What is it?"

"I don't think they are who they claim to be," she told him as they reached the top of the stairs.

"What do you mean?"

"I mean," she opened the office door and gasped.

"What is it?" he asked.

"The paper..." The desk was completely bare. The paper she'd printed with her evidence was missing.

"What paper?"

"I...I printed..." She stopped as she stared around the room. Someone had been in their house. Maybe two some-ones. Someone had taken the only evidence she had. But, the most chilling thing of all was that someone had known exactly where to find the evidence only seconds after she'd printed it.

There was only one explanation, and as she stared at her husband, she had no idea how to tell him the terrifying truth she'd just discovered.

They were being watched.

CHAPTER FORTY-THREE

BRYANT

Bryant stood on their front porch, watching the house next door with a sharp eye. It had a strange sense of foreboding, much less welcoming than it had originally seemed. Now that he knew the evil it held—*potentially* held—it was no longer a house that he dreamed of owning. Complete with a woman he had no idea why he'd ever found enticing.

The lights had been off all day, both cars gone. He'd watched carefully, trying to catch a light flickering on, or a curtain moving, but he hadn't. They weren't home. Why weren't they? Where were they?

Ever since Harper had told him what she discovered, his mind had been reeling. What other secrets were the Fullers hiding? Who were they, anyway? Where was the real Jason Fuller? They'd searched the internet fully, but with such a common name, their search was endless. Luckily, they'd been able to find the articles Harper was searching for—the first picture after the fire of the Jason they knew, and then the other of a completely different Jason Fuller.

Had the Jason they knew set the fire? Were they truly in

danger? He couldn't be sure, but he didn't need to be. What he needed was to get his wife and child away from this place, away from these people—once and for all.

Despite his fear of the neighbors, and what secrets they might be hiding, he couldn't deny the overwhelming sense of curiosity. If they could get in that house somehow, prove that they were being watched...maybe the police could do something about it. Maybe they wouldn't have to leave after all, if the neighbors left instead.

With that idea looming in his head, he pulled open the front door and called to his wife. "Harper, come here!"

She appeared within a few seconds, her worried eyes searching the room before they landed on him. "What? What is it?"

"I need your help with something."

She placed a hand to her chest, exhaling. "Nothing's wrong?"

"What? Oh, no. No, sorry."

"Okay, well, what is it, then?"

"Come here," he told her, ushering her out to the porch and speaking in hushed tones. "I want to break into Tori and Jason's house."

She scoffed, then, seeming to realize he was serious, shook her head. "No! No way. Why would you want to do that? Don't you realize how bad of an idea that is?"

"Yeah, I do," he said honestly, "but what choice do we have? Even with the house up for sale, it could be months before it sells. I can't live like this for months. I can't worry about what we say and do in our house. We've already said we can't afford both the house *and* an apartment in Chicago. Your parents don't really have the room, and we can't go without medical insurance for you and the baby while we both look for jobs there. It's too risky. But if we can find proof that they're spying on us...or that they're doing all of this crazy stuff, maybe we can get them arrested, and then we wouldn't have to worry about it. We could stay for as long as we had to."

"Okay, but what are you hoping to find? You think they have a secret lab with swabs of our hair and video camera feeds?" she asked with a half-laugh.

"Is this funny to you?" he asked. "Because you're the one who convinced me they're dangerous, remember?"

She swallowed. "Yes, of course I do. I just...this is crazy. It's so crazy. We aren't criminals, Bryant. Do you even know *how* to break into a house?"

"How hard can it be?"

"What if they have an alarm system? I'm pretty sure Tori said they do. Or cameras? What if they catch us?"

He bit his lip, trying to think. He was trying to remember what he'd seen when they'd been invited into the Fullers' home. They definitely seemed the type to have a security system, though there were no signs outside their home warning of one. "I don't know," he told his wife. "I guess it was a stupid idea."

"It wasn't stupid," Harper assured him—patronized him, more like it—quickly. "But it's not something we're capable of. Everything's going to be okay, even if we have to move in with my parents for a while. They may not have room, but you know they won't turn us away. I just want us to be safe."

"Me too," he agreed, taking her hands in his and kissing her fingers. "Me too. We're going to figure something out, I promise."

CHAPTER FORTY-FOUR

HARPER

When Harper arrived home from her doctor's appointment a week later, she knew something was up the moment she entered her house. The room was in disarray—pictures thrown everywhere, books pulled from bookshelves. Vents out of floors and walls, doors standing open.

She knelt down, grabbing hold of a heavy picture frame and walking further into the room. Someone was in her home. She could hear them moving around, shuffling through things. And she had a picture frame to protect herself. She wanted to run from the house—to dart out to find the safety of her car, but she needed to find out who was tormenting her. She needed to know the truth once and for all.

She walked up the stairs carefully, being extra cautious as she took each step. The office door was wide open, papers lying everywhere, but the room was empty. In the bedroom, the closet was open and she could hear the intruder breathing heavily. She walked slowly, raising the frame above her head—ready to strike should the moment call for it. As she eased herself around the corner of the closet, she took a half breath as the man turned to face her.

"What the he—"

"Bryant?" she cried, staring at her husband in disbelief.

"Harper? What are you doing?" He stepped out of her line of fire, though she was lowering the frame anyway.

"What am *I* doing? What are *you* doing? This house is a disaster! Were we robbed?"

"What?" He glanced around. "No. Look," he pulled her from the closet and toward the bed, "what I found."

Lying on the bed in a brown wicker basket, were three light switch covers. They were large and tan with screws threaded through them and drywall still stuck to the screws —as if they'd been ripped from the walls in an instant.

"What are these?" she asked, reaching for them.

"Don't touch," he insisted. "I did some research at school about finding hidden cameras in hotel rooms and stuff. Turns out it's as simple as using your phone and listening for feedback when you're on a call. So, I tried it today. The cameras are hidden in the ends of the screws. They sell this stuff on Amazon," he said angrily. "I guess I got a little carried away searching the rest of the house after I found these. But all that matters is that I found out how they've been watching us. I'm going to take these to the police."

The words hit her hard, and she took a step back, her lips quivering. "You...found hidden cameras...in our house?"

He nodded. "Yeah, in the office, the bedroom, and the living room. I'm still looking for more."

She sucked in a haggard breath. "What...why...are you sure?"

"Of course I'm sure."

"Should you have touched these? We need to call the police now."

He stared at the box, his expression falling flat. "Shit. I

175

didn't even think. I was just so...freaked out. Should I put them back?"

"No," she said plainly. "No, just don't touch them anymore. I'll call them now." She pulled her phone from her back pocket, searching for the non-emergency line, though this felt like somewhat of an emergency.

"How was the doctor?" Bryant asked. "I wish I could've come."

"It's okay," she said. "These are mostly boring appointments, anyway. You'll be at the ultrasound one." She offered him a small smile as she located the number and hit the button to call. "Baby is perfect."

───────

ONCE THE POLICE had searched the home for more video cameras—which they didn't find—they met Harper and Bryant back in the living room. They were perched on the edge of the couch, hands locked together on their knees.

The first officer—the one who'd introduced himself as Officer Riggs—cleared his throat. The couple stood quickly. Harper could feel her throat closing under his stern stares. "Everything looks clear. We searched the house for any type of video or audio feed, but it looks like the cameras you found must've been all that existed. We're going to take these down to the station to try and pull some fingerprints."

"What about our neighbors? Can't you go ahead and take them in?" Bryant asked.

The officer shook his head. "I'm sorry. I know you're convinced this was them, but without proof we don't even have enough to question them. Do you have anything else that would help support your claims?"

"We...I don't think they're telling the truth about who they are," Harper said, turning to walk into the kitchen. She grabbed the paper she'd printed for the second time off of the counter and walked back into the room, handing it over to the officer. "This is Jason Fuller. I believe our neighbor may have stolen his identity."

"That's a pretty serious accusation. Can you tell me why you believe that?"

"Because that's not him," she said firmly, pointing toward the paper. "Not the neighbor we know."

"It's not that uncommon of a name, Mrs. Page."

"I know, but—"

"Look, we'll look into it, but without something more concrete, there just isn't a whole lot we can do. Our best hope is that we find some prints on these cameras." He sighed, seeing their fallen expressions. "Have they threatened you in any way?"

"They may have broken in," Bryant offered. "But we don't know for sure."

"Someone was at our door the other day, and when Bryant got home, the door was open and that article was missing. And, once before, our phones were misplaced in the middle of the night," Harper said, though she was sure they'd already lost the officer's attention.

"Plus we keep getting all of this junk mail…stuff we didn't order," Bryant said.

"Bryant got mugged awhile back. We thought it was nothing, but they got a copy of our house key. It may be unrelated, but like he's saying, strange things keep happening. I am getting calls about appointments I didn't make. Bryant was even called for an interview for a position he didn't apply for a few days ago," Harper told him, recalling the strange phone call Bryant had received asking him to come in for an interview for a local garbage company. "It isn't just us, either. The old owner of this house even said they freaked her out, too."

"Did you get your locks changed after the mugging?" the officer asked.

"No," Bryant answered. "We will."

"You need to. Now, about the old owner, did they threaten her?"

"No," Bryant said softly.

"And you said they haven't threatened either of you?"

"No," came his answer.

"I'm sorry," the officer said after a brief pause. "I know this must be incredibly frustrating. You have to understand that our job is to look at facts, and without anything more solid...it's just your word against theirs. There's nothing we can do unless you have concrete proof that your neighbors are the ones harassing you. If they threaten you, we can get an order of protection."

"What? Like a piece of paper? You can't arrest them?"

"Let's take this one step at a time, okay?" he said, putting a hand on Bryant's shoulder. "For now, just keep your doors locked. Get those locks changed. You're safe here for the night. There are no more cameras. You aren't being watched. Keep the curtains drawn and call us if anything happens. I'll be in touch as soon as we get the prints back from the cameras." He picked up the evidence bag of light switch covers and tucked them under his arm. "You guys take care."

As he disappeared through their doorway, Harper watched his car descend down their drive, the feeling of safety leaving with him.

"I don't want to stay here," she said, turning to face her husband.

He closed his eyes, exhaling. "We'll be out of here soon."

"How can you be sure?" she asked.

"I'll call the realtor in the morning and ask if she's had anyone call about it. Even if we have to give the house away, we just need it gone." He kissed her forehead. "I'm not going to let anything happen to you."

She jumped, letting out a scream as someone knocked on the door. As she turned around, she stared into the face that had been filling her nightmares. Jason Fuller—or whoever he truly was.

CHAPTER FORTY-FIVE

HARPER

J ason stood just beyond the screen door, his eyes burning into the couple. Just behind him stood Tori. Harper hadn't seen her at first glance, her black jumpsuit blending in with the night around her, but soon enough she was able to make out her porcelain skin and high ponytail of blonde hair.

Harper looked at Bryant, who was staring at Jason with a stern jaw. "What do you want?" he asked through the glass.

"Are you guys okay?" Jason asked. "We saw the cop car. Wanted to check on you."

"Do you mean you wanted to spy on us again?" Bryant asked. "There's no chance in hell we're letting you in, so you can either go away or we'll call the cops back."

"What are you talking about?" Jason asked. "Why would we be spying on you? We just happened to notice the cop car leaving the driveway, that's not exactly spying."

"We know all about what you've been up to," Bryant argued.

"We found the cameras," Harper added.

Jason stared at her, his head cocked to the side in confusion.

Tori pursed her lips, sneering. "If anyone's been spying, Bryant, it's you. But I had enough class to let that go. If you're going to go around accusing us of such ridiculous things, I won't be so polite."

"What is she talking about?" Harper asked, glancing over her shoulder at Bryant, whose face was turning bright red.

"Now's not the time," he said firmly, but his eyes were locked on Tori. When Harper looked back to her, her face held a slight smirk.

"What? You don't want me to tell all your dirty little secrets?" she teased.

Jason looked at her, his expression filled with fury. "Tori, not now."

"What is going on?" Harper asked, suddenly feeling like she was the only one not in on their collective secret.

"Just ignore her," Jason said.

"I hardly think I'm the one you should be mad at, baby," Tori told Jason, touching his cheek. "I'm the only one who seems to be telling the truth around here."

"You need to leave," Bryant said, stepping in front of Harper. "Before we call the police."

"You wouldn't dare—"

"We already have—"

"You mother—"

"Stop it!" Harper yelled, hands up in the air to her sides. "I want to know what you're talking about." She reached for the door handle on the screen door without allowing herself to reconsider. "Come inside."

Without waiting for a further invitation, Tori stormed past Jason, who looked apprehensive at best as he entered the house. "Tor, this isn't the time. Let's just go."

Tori smiled at her husband, though the smile was filled

with venom. "I think we all have a lot to discuss, and if we're going to make this work…well, we'll have to work together, won't we? We're going to be a family, after all." Her lips pursed as she placed an arm on the edge of their mantle, and Harper noticed for the first time how her hand rubbed across the lower part of her abdomen.

CHAPTER FORTY-SIX

HARPER

"A family?" Harper asked, reaching for the edge of the couch. Jason reached for her instinctively, and she pulled away, slipping and landing on the floor. Bryant was still staring at Tori in disbelief as Jason reached his hand out to help Harper up.

"Here," he said softly. His eyes were kind—the way she'd remembered. She took his hand, letting him lift her up. Her husband's eyes never left Tori.

"You're…you're pregnant?" Harper asked.

"I thought you knew," Jason said, his brow furrowed. "When I asked if you knew…you said you did."

"When did you ask me?" she demanded.

"When I came over the other day…"

"That's what you were talking about? I thought you just meant the affair. How would I have known about the pregnancy?"

"I assumed he told you," Tori said firmly.

"You knew?" Harper asked Bryant, her body on fire with fury as she stared at the dumbfounded, guilty look on his face. "How could you not tell me?"

"I don't trust them, Harp. I don't trust that it's mine. We've only had sex twice. How can you be sure it's not his? You planned this all along, didn't you?" he demanded, standing up to face Tori.

She didn't flinch as he moved closer, unwavering in her power. "Planned what?" she dared him, and Harper saw Bryant's eyes dart toward her before he swallowed.

"You have no idea that the baby is mine, if there even is a baby," he said hatefully.

"It'll be easy enough to prove once it's born," Tori said coldly.

"What do you want from us?" Bryant demanded, his voice shaking. Whether it was shaking from fear or anger, Harper couldn't tell.

"In the beginning? Your friendship," Tori answered. "But at this point? We really don't know that you're worth it. But this baby is yours, Bryant. So, I do expect you to be a part of its life."

"You're okay with this?" Harper asked Jason, trying to keep her voice low.

"Like I said before," Jason said, his voice a low growl, "we've been together long enough to know when we see something better. I knew what would happen the moment you two moved in." He didn't sound entirely fine with what was happening, but what choice did he have? What choice did she have? Bryant and Tori were leading the show, and it was obvious she and Jason were going to be expected to go along with it.

"Well, we're moving. We're selling the house," Harper said, attempting to regain some power. Was that even true anymore? Would Bryant leave Tori knowing what he knew?

"We noticed the sign," Jason said. "But it won't sell quickly. It's likely you'll still be here when the babies are born."

"Babies?" Harper asked, shocked by his words. "As in…twins?"

Jason scowled. "No. As in, both babies. Yours and ours."

"So you did know that I'm pregnant, then?" Harper asked, something she hadn't confirmed completely before then.

"The nurse congratulated me when we left the hospital that day. She assumed I was the father."

"But…you didn't say anything?"

"It wasn't my place," he told her. "And it wasn't any of my business. I thought we were friends…all of us. But I see now that I was wrong." He reached for Tori's hand. "That *we* were wrong."

Tori's eyes met Harper's suddenly, full of disdain. "Apparently so."

Harper furrowed her brow. "I could never be friends with someone like you. You slept with my husband."

"It takes two," she said simply. "And from what Jay has said, you were only a few minutes alone with him from doing the same."

"Tori—" Jason said angrily.

"What?" Bryant yelled at the same time. "You were going to sleep with him?"

"No!" she exclaimed. "Of course not. We just kissed—"

"Kissed?" Bryant demanded. "You *kissed* him?"

"Like you have room to talk," Jason said hatefully.

"Please just go," Harper begged. "Please. We don't need this right now." She clutched her stomach for emphasis.

Jason sighed, looking her over. "Look, she's right. We need to go. We don't have to figure this all out right now. This was not why we came over here. We just…wanted to check on you. But, obviously we aren't welcome." He pulled Tori's hand, leading her toward the door.

"Good night, Harper," he said to her. "Good night, Bryant."

"Good night, Jason," Harper said, "or whoever you are." The words slipped from her tongue, surprising everyone including herself. His eyes locked with hers, and she knew in that moment that he knew what she meant. He stood, frozen, studying her for a few seconds before he blinked and looked down.

As she shut the door, he looked back up, his eyes were locking back with hers through the screened door and then the beveled glass of the wooden door. His expression said it all. It told her everything she needed to know. She'd discovered something big, whether the police believed her or not.

As their shadows finally left their doorway, Harper released a breath she hadn't meant to be holding.

CHAPTER FORTY-SEVEN

BRYANT

The next morning, Bryant climbed out of bed at the first sign of light. He hadn't slept at all—his mind racing all night long—which had given him plenty of time to sort everything out.

The first, and most important, thing he needed to do was to call their realtor. He pulled his phone from the charger, scrolling through his contacts until he saw her name. He clicked on it, listening to it ring a few times before her groggy sounding voice came across the line. He'd obviously woken her up.

"Joan Walden Real Estate, how may I help you?"

"Hey, Joan, it's Bryant Page. From Lancaster Mills."

"Hi, Bryant, how are you?" she asked.

"I was just calling to see how many people we've had interested in the house. You haven't done any showings yet. We're considering lowering the price."

She made a 'hmm' noise and cleared her throat. "How *many?* None yet. You could lower the price if you want, but I'd suggest leaving it at the price we have listed for a few months."

"*Months?*" he exclaimed, shocked by her words. "What do you mean months?"

"Bryant, the house was listed for four years before you guys came along." She let out a soft chuckle. "I'm sorry. I'll do everything I can to get it sold for you, but the fact is that no one is moving to Lancaster Mills. You aren't in Chicago anymore."

His heart raced as she said the words he would've never guessed could be coming. "We don't have years to wait. We need to sell this house, like…yesterday."

"I understand," she said, "and I promise you I'm doing all I can. But, it's not going to happen overnight. It's a rural area. I sell a house or two a month on a good month, and that's within five towns. I'll get the house sold for you guys, but you're going to have to be patient with it, okay?"

He groaned. "Thanks, Joan."

"Don't get discouraged, okay? It's going to be fine."

He nodded, though she couldn't see him. "Thanks."

When he slid his phone back onto the dresser and looked over, Harper's eyes were open, staring at him. "Not good news?" she asked, though she seemed to already know the answer.

"We're going to figure it out," he promised.

She nodded. "Are we going to talk about…last night?" She wouldn't meet his eye as she asked the question he'd known was coming.

"There's no way she could know that the baby is mine, Harp."

"But what if it is?" she asked. "How long were you planning to keep that secret from me?"

"I…don't know."

"Would you want to be a part of its life?"

"I don't know what I want," he said, sinking into the bed and patting her leg. "Besides you. And us. And *our* baby.

That's what I'm certain about. The rest...it's too hard to figure out."

She pulled her leg away from him. "I don't know what I want either," she said firmly. "But I want to get out of here. For good. I don't care if we have to foreclose. I don't care anymore. I can't stand to be here. I can't stand to watch her and think about what you did. I made my decision last night. I'm going back to Chicago."

"You know we can't afford to—"

"Me, Bryant. I'm going. On my own." She swallowed, finally looking up to meet his eyes. "You can do what you want. It's your mess to clean up, anyway."

"You're leaving me?" he asked, his eyes burning with sudden tears.

To his dismay, she didn't deny it instantly. "I thought I was okay with this. I thought I could...learn to be okay with it. To accept what you did and to move on. But, last night made it clear that I can't. That we'll always be running from your mistakes. When you cheated on me, I thought it would kill me. But somehow I made it through," she said, tears forming in her eyes. "But last night, when Tori said she was pregnant, the wound was ripped open again. I can't do this anymore, Bryant. I can't," she took a sharp breath, "I just can't do it."

"You know that I love you," he said, reaching to cup her cheek.

She grasped his hand, moving it from her face slowly. Her expression wasn't angry, but full of sorrow. He wasn't sure which would hurt worse. "I do know that," she told him with a nod. "And I love you, too. But, it's not just about that anymore. I want to be the best momma to this little baby, and I'm not sure I can do that in this situation. I need time to figure everything out. Which means I need time away from this place...and from you."

He swallowed, looking away as he attempted to blink the tears back from his eyes. "Okay," he said finally, unable to form even one more word.

Harper slid her legs out from under the covers, walking past him as her hand grazed his shoulder. He watched her walk out the door, knowing she may as well have been walking away from him for good. It was only a matter of time before she realized she was better off without him. She always had been. His life had been one screw up after the other—until her. Until she brought light into his world. It was only fitting he'd managed to mess that up, too.

He lay down where she had been, pulling the covers up to his chest. He'd made his bed, he may as well lie in it.

CHAPTER FORTY-EIGHT

HARPER

That night, Harper woke up on the couch. Truth was, she hadn't been sleeping well, and she couldn't decide if it was the entire situation, the ever-growing baby resting on her bladder, or the lumpy couch that was causing most of her distress.

As she rolled over, trying to stand up, she was reminded again of just how much her body was changing by the day. She stood, walking up the stairs quietly with one hand resting on her growing belly. She rushed into the bathroom, emptying her bladder with sleep-filled eyes.

When she was done, she wandered into the office, wanting to check and see if there was an earlier flight available than the one she'd booked this morning. She needed one for that day, if possible, because she couldn't run on such little sleep for much longer.

She opened the browser, watching as it took her to the last open page—Bryant's email. There was one unopened email from Donna Brooks, the woman who had sold them their home. Out of curiosity, Harper clicked on it, reading through the email.

No, it read, **I never really had any trouble out of them. They tend to keep to themselves. Is everything okay?**

Harper cocked her head to the side, reading over the message once again. She searched for the sent message that she'd been replying to but didn't see it. She clicked the button labeled 'Inbox' on the far left hand side of her screen and searched through his messages. Hadn't he just told her that Donna said she always felt like something was strange with them? That she felt like they were watching her?

There. Seven messages down was another message, also from Donna Brooks. **I did my best to stay away from them...they just always seemed odd to me. They knew things they shouldn't have known, like they were watching me or something. My advice? Keep far away.**

She read the message he'd sent her: **Donna, my name is Bryant Page. My wife and I recently purchased and moved into your home in Lancaster Mills. We are truly loving it here but we are having some issues with the neighbors— Jason and Tori Fuller. I was wondering if you could give me some insight into them? Did you ever have any issues? Any info would be greatly appreciated.**

So, Donna had told him at first that there were problems and then later responded that there were none. What did that mean? Why would she change her mind so suddenly?

Out of the corner of her eye, something caught her attention. She turned her head toward the window and gasped. *No.*

CHAPTER FORTY-NINE

HARPER

Harper dashed down the stairs as quickly as she could run. She grabbed her phone from the end table near the couch.

"Bryant!" she called up the stairs, yelling at her sleeping husband as she darted out the door, dialing 911 with shaking hands.

"Hello, 911, what's your emergency?"

"I...there's a fire." She stared up at the flames in front of her, heat from the blaze warming her skin as smoke filled the air. How long had the Fullers' house been on fire? How had it started? The house was nearly completely black, charred from the inside out as the flames continued to grow and climb, bringing large parts of the house down easily with loud crashes.

"Jason! Tori!" she called, trying to get as close to the fire as possible without endangering her life. *Please, God, don't let them still be in there.*

She stepped back as she listened to the dispatcher's calm voice on the line, requesting her address and trying to let her know help was on the way. She held onto the phone, her heart pounding as she watched the disaster unfold in horror. She had fallen to her knees, though she couldn't remember when it happened, the phone beside her in the grass as cool tears collected on her cheeks. She'd never witnessed anything so terrible—for a girl who'd grown up in Chicago, that was saying something. She took short, sharp breaths, trying her best to maintain composure.

When another section of the once beautiful house collapsed, sending ashes and soot toward her, she lunged backward, landing face first in the dirt. She watched as Bryant's house shoes came hurrying toward her from the porch.

"Are you okay?" he demanded, scooping her up. "Jesus Christ, Harp, what happened?" As she looked up at him, his eyes were on the neighbors' house, watching as it continued to burn.

"We need to go in there," she said, staring at the reflection of the flames in the vehicles in their driveway. "Tori and Jason could still be inside."

"Are you crazy?" Bryant asked. "You're pregnant. You aren't going anywhere. We need to call the police."

"I already did," she told him, looking around for her phone. She spied the light in the grass, walking over to it and picking it up. A few neighbors down the road had started coming out onto their porches, and suddenly she filled with relief as she heard the sirens assuring her that help was on the way.

She watched as two fire trucks pulled up, their sirens still blaring as they stopped in front of the house, and the men began to climb out of the trucks. They moved quickly, talking to no one as they went to work, trying and failing to put out the large flames.

They were clad in their suits, and Harper watched in awe as they bravely fought their way closer and closer toward the flame. A man approached her, his helmet off. "Do you know if anyone is inside?" he asked.

"We have neighbors that live there," she told him. "A man and woman about our age. I don't know if they were home or not, but their cars are there."

The man nodded, turning and running back toward the house. He threw on his helmet, grabbed another fireman, and together they made their way into the house.

Harper covered her mouth in horror, holding her breath as she waited to see them emerge. She may not like Tori and Jason, but the thought of them dying—the thought of them dying like this—was enough to make her sick.

Bryant stood behind her, his hands caressing her arms. "It's going to be okay," he whispered in her ear. "They'll find them."

She couldn't help noticing the way he held her extra close, and she wondered if he wished it were Tori in his arms instead.

CHAPTER FIFTY

HARPER

An hour later, Harper remained on her front porch. Bryant was beside her, his arms still around her as he continued to hand her bits of the toast he had made. Her stomach was upset, for obvious reasons, and even the medicine for her morning sickness didn't seem to be helping.

The flames had finally been calmed, though the house had collapsed completely into a pile of rubble in the process. The street was lined with cop cars and police tape as the officers worked to keep people away while the firemen continued to spray charred wood. It was just... gone. All of it. Everything that had once made their neighbors' home so beautiful had disintegrated in a matter of minutes.

They were the only ones allowed on this side of the tape, the only ones who could see what was happening, thanks to the proximity of their house to the disaster. They'd been watching carefully for the body bags, the ones Harper knew would be coming, but so far, there'd been nothing.

The men were still searching through the wreckage, and though she knew they still had a long way to go, she couldn't help but hope that they'd see Tori and Jason pulling down the driveway, devastated about their loss, but alive nonetheless.

"Here, eat another bite," Bryant whispered, taking one for himself as he pinched off a piece of toast and handed it to her.

"Thanks," she said, taking the bread cautiously. She couldn't take her eyes off the house—or lack thereof—next door. Where were their neighbors?

A fireman approached their house, his face covered in soot. "Do you have a way to contact your neighbors?" he asked. "See if they maybe went out for the night?"

"You still haven't found anything?" Harper asked.

Bryant pulled out his phone, scrolling through his contacts. *Of course he had Tori's number.*

"Not yet," he said. "But we're not done searching."

"Do you know what caused it?" Harper asked.

"We won't know until the fire marshal does a full investigation. Did you guys see anything suspicious?"

"No," Harper said. "By the time I noticed, the house was already up in flames."

Just then, a police officer appeared from behind the fireman, and Harper recognized him instantly as the officer who'd taken the cameras from their house just a day ago.

"Mr. and Mrs. Page, how are you?"

"Fine, Officer," Harper said, trying hard to remember his name.

"This is tragic, isn't it?" he asked.

"It really is," Bryant said. "Here's her number. Tori's." He held out his phone to the fireman.

"Could you call her?" he asked.

Bryant nodded, placing the phone to his ear. They stood, watching him as he listened to the line ringing. After a moment, he put his phone down. "No answer."

"Thanks for your help, guys. Just…let us know if you hear

anything back," the fireman said, turning to walk back toward the house's remains.

After a minute, the officer frowned, watching the fireman leave and then turning back to Bryant and Harper. "Could I, um, could I get you guys to come with me for a bit?"

"Come with you?" Harper asked, standing up as the officer motioned for them to. "What for?"

"We just need to ask you some questions down at the station."

"About what?" Bryant asked.

"About the fire," he said calmly. "We know you've been having problems with your neighbors...so you can understand why this might seem suspicious."

"You think *we* started it?" Harper asked. "Why would we? We were the ones being threatened and stalked by them!"

"We just need to ask you a few questions, Mrs. Page. Just as a formality. Right now, we don't even know if the cause was arson."

"Of course," Harper said obligingly, trying to calm her racing heart. *Where were the neighbors?*

CHAPTER FIFTY-ONE

HARPER

A week later, the news announced that the Fullers' bodies still had not been located, and since no one had heard from them, they were officially labeled as 'missing.' The house next door still lay in a blackened heap surrounded by police tape that was beginning to split in the wind. They had to be dead, right? Their cars were still there. No one had seen or heard from them since that night. Somehow, deep down, Harper just knew that their bodies were going to be discovered soon. As tragic as it was, she couldn't help hoping it would be sooner than later, ready to be rid of the anxiety that had been gnawing at her continuously.

She texted Bryant at work, letting him know the news. She wasn't sure how she should feel about it. Relieved because they could stay in Lancaster Mills now without worry about their neighbors, sad because their lives had been ended unnecessarily, scared because the cause of the fire still hadn't been determined, or worried because if the fire was ruled arson, the police had made it incredibly clear that they would be the prime suspects. It was why she was still in

Lancaster Mills in the first place. If she left now, she'd look even more suspicious.

When she didn't receive a response back from Bryant, she wasn't immediately worried because she knew it was sometimes hard for him to check his phone. Two hours later, when her phone rang and the number wasn't one she knew, she slid her finger across the screen apprehensively. "Hello?"

"Harper?" he asked, his voice low.

"Bryant? What number is this?" She had the school's number saved in her phone.

"The police station," he said. "I've been arrested."

Her heart plummeted at his words. "Arrested? What do you mean? Why?"

"Because of what happened with Tori and Jason. The fire. I'm in big trouble. I need you to ask your parents to borrow money. I'm going to need a lawyer. Can you please come?"

She took a breath, hearing the words she never expected in a thousand years. "O-okay. Let me call them. Are you okay?"

"I'm okay," he said. "Please don't leave while I'm in here. I know you're supposed to be going to Chicago once the investigation is over, but...I need you."

"I'm here," she said softly.

"I love you," he told her.

"You too," she said. "I'll be there soon, okay?" With that, she pressed the button to end the call, going to the search engine on her phone to look up a lawyer in town. She'd never needed to hire a lawyer and wasn't sure exactly what to expect. How much money would she need? Would her parents even be able to help her? She looked around the too-empty house, feeling incredibly alone and hating how far away from her family she was.

As she clicked on the first listing, she heard something above her head. She froze, lifting her ear toward the ceiling to listen closer. After a moment, she heard it again. Someone was upstairs.

She stood. She could hear them. Moving. Pacing. Something was being shuffled around. She dialed 911, holding her finger above the button to place the call as she walked up the stairs carefully, her toes cold on the hardwood flooring.

She kept her breaths short and quick, trying not to make too much noise as she rounded the corner and came face to face with her intruder.

She let her phone drop to her side. "It's you."

CHAPTER FIFTY-TWO

HARPER

"I —I don't...understand," she said, pacing the room frantically. "How are you here right now? How are you alive? What are you doing in my house?"

Jason shook his head, setting down the stack of papers in his hand. "How did you know about me?" he asked.

"What are you talking about?"

"The other night...you said 'Jason or whoever you are.' What did you mean by that?"

She took a step back as he moved closer. "What do you think I meant?"

"What do you know about me?" he demanded, his voice growing angrier.

"I was right, then, wasn't I? You aren't Jason Fuller," she said it with a confidence she didn't entirely have. "Who are you? And where is he?"

"How could you possibly know that?" he asked, scratching his head as he looked out the window to where their house had once stood.

"I...I found an article online. The picture wasn't you. I'm

x

sorry…why are you in my house right now? And why haven't you told the police you aren't dead yet? Where is Tori? *Bryant was just arrested for your murder.*" She felt relief hit her stomach as she realized this was just all some mistake. Everything was going to be okay. *As long as Jason wasn't there to kill her*—she pushed the thought from her head. She didn't feel threatened around him, even now. Somehow she just seemed to know she was safe.

When Jason looked away from the window and met her eyes, he looked truly shocked. "I'm sorry, Harper. That was never our intention. None of this."

"What are you talking about?"

"I can't stay. I'm sorry."

"How did you even get in here, Jason? Why do you keep breaking into my house?"

"The back door was unlocked," he explained. He glanced at the watch on his wrist. "Look, I don't have much time. Tori'd kill me if she knew I was here. I just…I wanted to apologize for everything. I wanted to tell you—to beg you—never to tell anyone what you know about me."

"But I don't know anything about you. And you can't leave now. You have to go tell the police that you aren't dead. Otherwise Bryant won't be able to come home."

He patted the air with his hand frantically. "I'm sorry. I really am, but I can't do that. The police can't know that I'm alive. I died in that fire, Harper, just like I died in a fire fourteen years ago."

"What are you talking about?" she demanded, stepping in front of him as he moved to leave. "You need to tell me the truth. You have to help me fix this."

"I don't have time for that," he said. "I—look, I truly am sorry. I came here to tell you—to warn you, to forget whatever you know."

"What were you looking for?"

"I was trying to see if you had proof about who I am. I wanted to know what you knew."

"But I don't know anything...except who you aren't."

"You don't know anything, Harper. You can't." He touched her shoulder, his lips pressed into a thin line of regret. "I wish I could tell you more, but I can't. Tori would be furious."

"She controls you, doesn't she? Just because she's beautiful, you do everything she says? You let her sleep with whoever she wants? You let her get pregnant by another man? A *married* man?" Her lips curled in disgust.

He glanced at his watch again. "I'm sorry, Harper. I've really got to go." He let go of her shoulder, darting past her. She let out a heavy breath, shaking her head. When she turned around, he was still there, staring at her from the hallway. "I know you want to help Bryant, but...meet me tonight, okay?"

"Meet you? What are you talking about?"

"Meet me tonight at seven by the Fourteenth Avenue pier in Myrtle Beach. I'll tell you everything." Before she could answer, or even think about her answer, he was walking away. And with him, her hope disappeared. She needed to help Bryant...but first, she needed to know the truth.

THAT EVENING, she walked across the sand, its warmth heating her skin as she made her way toward the pier. She'd worn a casual white dress, unsure of whether she should be dressed up or down. *Not that it should matter.* Her hair danced in the wind, blowing into her eyes as she searched for him.

She grew closer to the pier, watching as tourists and locals alike ran past her, everyone captivated by the beautiful evening in front of them. Everyone except her. Because she had a mission. And as she reached the pier, her target stood in front of her.

"Hi," he said softly, running a hand over his blue shirt nervously. He'd chosen khaki shorts and a button down shirt —so, it seemed he was having the same dilemma she had been. Not too dressed up or down. *But it didn't matter.* "I, um, I didn't know if you'd come."

"If I'm being honest, I probably shouldn't have."

"I'm glad you did," he told her. Before she had time to process his words, he turned away from her, beginning to walk along the shore. He waved over his shoulder for her to follow. She took off her sandals, carrying them in her hand so she could keep up.

"So, what are you going to tell me?" she asked. The salt water splashed against her ankles, and she realized it was the first time she'd ever been at the beach with so much stress built up in her—any stress, really. The ocean tended to bring her peace, but tonight was different.

"I don't really know where to start," he said, looking straight ahead with a stern expression. They continued to walk as she contemplated what to say next. "Well, I guess the first thing you should know is that Bryant didn't start the fire. And he certainly didn't kill me or Tori. We're both alive and well." He cleared his throat. "Well, alive at least."

Harper looked over her shoulder. "Where is she?"

He shrugged. "I don't know, honestly. We went our separate ways. We both needed…space."

"What? You're going to get divorced?"

"Dead people can't get divorced, Harper."

"I don't understand."

He nodded. "I know that. And…even once I explain it, you probably won't. But, I want to tell you anyway. Because I think you deserve to know the truth. Even if you use it against me."

"The truth about the fact that you aren't Jason Fuller?" she asked.

He paused before shaking his head firmly. "No. I am not Jason Fuller."

"So who are you?" she asked.

He turned, facing the water and stopping their walk suddenly. His hands went into his pockets as he began to speak. "My name is—was—Roy Breeland."

The name struck her, and she tried to remember why it seemed so familiar.

"When I was fifteen, the foster house where I lived burned down. Eleven people died. My foster parents and my foster brothers and sisters."

She gasped, though it was something she realized she should've probably already pieced together. "You were in foster care with Tori."

He nodded. "I was. But, when the fire department came, and the police asked my name...Tori didn't give them mine. She said I was Jason."

"But why?"

He kicked a bit of sand out in front of them. "See, I was only fifteen at the time, which means Tori and I would've gone back into foster care after the fire. But...Jason was eighteen. He was legally an adult. An adult who was dead. They were all dead. We saw our way out, after a lifetime of horrible foster homes. The Fullers were the first decent people we'd ever lived with. I mean, they were a little odd, but we were getting food regularly, they weren't beating us or molesting us. They were good people. The fire...well, it took that tiny sense of safety from us once again. So, we acted impulsively and, somehow, we got away with it."

"Didn't anyone know what Jason looked like? Relatives?"

"The Fullers' parents had already passed, and they were only children. So, no aunts or uncles. They were all homeschooled, so the kids—Jason included—didn't have many friends. Our social worker had just retired, and we were in the process of getting transferred to someone new. It shouldn't have worked…honestly, it was a stupid plan, but somehow it did. All of our stuff burned up in the fire. So, I just had to ask for a new birth certificate, social security card, driver's license…all of it. And, by some miracle, I was handed a new life."

"So, you took Tori in?"

He nodded. "I did. I petitioned a judge to let her stay in my custody until she turned eighteen. We just had a little over a year to go. After that, we moved here, far away from the only place we'd ever been known, and started over. There was a life insurance policy for the Fullers that went to me. It's how Tori afforded medical school, how we bought the house and her gym. It's how we got our fresh start. We built a life based on lies and somehow…it all just worked. So, when you said you knew I wasn't Jason Fuller, it freaked us out. Tori panicked. She said we had to disappear. Like before."

"Wait…are you telling me…did *you* start the fire?"

He looked at her then, his eyes filled with grief. "We had to make you think we'd died. We couldn't chance you telling anyone what you knew."

"So, if that was the reason…why are you telling me the truth now?"

He bit his lip. "Partially because you caught me in your house." He paused. "And partially because I can't seem to stay away from you."

She inhaled sharply. "You couldn't just tell me all of this? I would've kept your secret."

"Tori doesn't trust you," he said simply. "She…she finds it hard to trust anyone, honestly, and with the life we've lived, I can't say that I blame her."

"But she just left you? Disappeared? After all you did for her?"

He closed his eyes, grimacing. "Look, there's one more thing...and it's going to freak you out."

"More than everything you've already told me?" She scoffed.

"Tori and I aren't just foster siblings...we're...*sibling,* siblings."

"What?" she asked, her jaw dropping. Her lips curled as she realized what he was telling her. "You *married* your sister?"

"We never *legally* got married. She changed her name to keep up pretenses, but we never wanted to do too much to draw eyes toward us. We pretended to be married because we needed each other. Our whole lives we'd only had each other, and it was terrifying to think about starting over in a whole new place all alone. It was just...easy."

"I don't understand how that could possibly be easy."

"I know," he said. "I really do. But it was. It was simple and the best arrangement we could've hoped for...until you and Bryant moved in next door."

She sucked in a breath. "What are you talking about?"

"Look, Lancaster Mills isn't exactly a dating hub, and Tori stayed with me because of everything I'd sacrificed for her and for us. I could never legally get married for fear that someone would find out who I really was, so she didn't marry, either. She protected me just as much as I protected her. Then...this beautiful woman moved in next door and I... I found myself going crazy over her." He reached up, moving a piece of hair from her eyes and sliding his palm down her arm. "Tori saw it...she knew I liked you. She knew I would never act on it, but she saw an opening with Bryant and she went for it. For me, but for her, too. She'd always wanted the real deal someday. Real marriage. Kids of her own. She could never have that with me. We talked about fostering, but do you know how much digging they do into your background? Too much. Adoption, too. It was risky. I know you may not understand it, but you guys were our way out. You were the happiness we'd been waiting for. Tori wasn't trying to hurt you, Harper. She just wanted me to be happy. She deserved to be happy, too."

"But...Bryant and I...we were happy. Don't you see that? You ruined everything for us."

"Bryant cheated on you," he said. "He cheated on you, and now Tori's pregnant because of it."

She sucked in a breath. "And now he's in jail because of your plan."

"I never wanted that to happen. I swear to you I didn't. We used accelerant inside the house. I can't understand why they would blame Bryant. But I will do everything I can to help you fix it. Everything short of coming forward with my story." He shook his head. "I'm sorry, but I cannot do that."

"But, what about all the strange stuff that happened? The cameras in our house? The subscriptions? Abortion appointments? The slashed tires? The break-ins? That wasn't you guys?"

"What? Of course not! Why on earth would we do any of that? We liked you guys." He furrowed his brow, seeming genuinely confused.

"Because someone did," she said. "And if it wasn't you guys, then who was it?"

"I have no idea, Harper. Honestly, I don't. We truly did want to be your friends. Well, a little more than that, since I'm being honest."

"Friends don't sleep with their friend's husband, Jason. What you guys did...you really hurt me."

He pulled his hand back, squeezing his eyes shut. "I'm really sorry, Harper. I am. I never meant to hurt you. Tori never meant to hurt you. I guess we forgot there were real feelings involved. We, well, we kind of lost touch with reality. Fourteen years of a fake marriage will do that to you. And… well, I thought you liked me back."

"I was married, Jason. Still *am* married. As in…not available."

"I'm really sorry," he said again.

"So, what now?"

"What do you mean?"

"What are you going to do? Where are you going to go?"

"Well," he said, "I guess that depends on what comes next for you." His brown eyes searched hers, looking for an answer she could not give. It didn't matter how she felt about him. It didn't matter that he had once given her butterflies she couldn't deny. The fact was, after all the damage he'd done, all the pain he'd caused her…she couldn't feel those things anymore.

She had a very real husband and a very real child that she had to protect. She couldn't play pretend with Jason—Roy—whoever he'd be now.

"I have to go help Bryant."

"You don't have feelings for me?" he asked, a confirmation.

"That's not what I said. I don't know you. You helped me. You've been kind to me. But, you've also caused me a lot of pain. I know that wasn't your intention, but there's no future for us, Jason, if that's what you're asking me. I'm married. I have a child." She rested her hands on her stomach. "I'm sorry you gave up so much for me."

He nodded, staring across the ocean as the sun began to fade from view. "I'd do it all again," he promised, and his eyes said he meant it. "Just promise me one thing?"

"What's that?"

His shoulders raised in a drawn-out shrug. "Ask yourself

this, Harper Page, does he look at you the way that I do? Because I've seen him look at you…and I don't think you want to hear that answer."

She shook her head, feeling slighted by his honesty. "I don't…you can't…I have to go."

He nodded, and she could swear she saw small tears brimming his eyes as he cleared his throat and began to walk away. "Have a good life, Harper," he called, and for a moment she thought he was being catty. When he looked back over his shoulder one last time, his eyes were filled with sincerity. "You deserve it."

CHAPTER FIFTY-THREE

HARPER

Harper walked into the house with her phone in her hand. She had played the recording she'd made over and over on her way home. It was crystal clear, except for the occasionally swishing sound of her dress across the microphone. She had it. She had them. She could prove, once and for all, that Jason and Tori had planned the whole thing. That Bryant was innocent.

Then, once Bryant was safe and their family was back together, they could move home to Chicago or decide to stay in Lancaster Mills—it didn't matter because their family would once again be safe. Jason and Tori were gone forever. Never to darken their doorstep ever again.

She walked up the stairs of the quiet home, pulling her dress off and climbing into the shower. As the water washed over her, she thought about everything she had learned, still trying to piece together some parts of the mystery. If what Jason had said was true and the Fullers weren't the ones trying to harass them, then who had it been? None of it made any sense.

On top of that, she couldn't deny the flush that was still

on her cheeks from being in Jason's presence. Did she have feelings for him? Of course. But could she act on them? Never.

She was married. He'd been married to his sister. Okay, not legally, and not necessarily in a creepy way—his intentions had been noble, but he and his "wife" had schemed to break up a marriage. They'd caused her husband to cheat. Effectively, they'd ruined her life. She could never forgive that.

THE NEXT MORNING, Harper walked up the steps to the police station, recording in hand. She entered through the metal detectors, headed toward the front desk where an officer was waiting.

"Can I help you?"

"I'm here to see my husband."

"What's his name?"

"Bryant Page."

"Just a second," the woman said.

"I need to see an officer who's working on his case as well."

"Sure," the officer said, nodding her head as she picked up the phone.

After a few moments, another police officer appeared. "Mrs. Page?" he asked, waving his hand for her to follow him. She did as she was told, following him down a long hallway. "I'm Officer Rigdon. One of the officers on your husband's case. I'm sure the news came as quite a shock to you."

"Yes, it did. Actually, I wanted to talk to you. I have proof that my husband didn't commit the murders."

The officer stopped in his tracks, staring at her strangely. "Excuse me?"

"I—I have proof. My husband didn't kill Jason and Tori Fuller."

The officer smiled slightly, as if he thought she was joking. "Yeah, we know that."

"You do?" she asked, her jaw dropping as her grip on her phone lightened.

"Yeah. Mrs. Page, your husband wasn't arrested for murder. The accelerant found in the fire in the Fullers' home was found inside the home. Most likely an insurance scheme gone wrong." He shook his head. "Didn't your husband tell you what was going on?"

She swallowed, her throat suddenly feeling extremely dry. "I...I guess not. What do you—" As she began to speak, they turned down another corner and she spotted Bryant in a small cell, leaning against the bars.

"Oh, thank God it's you," he called to her as soon as he saw her.

Forgetting her conversation with the officer, she rushed forward, clutching her husband through the bars. "Are you okay?" she asked, leaning her forehead into his.

He nodded. "I'm so sorry about all of this."

"I...I don't understand," she said. "They said you aren't here for murder. So, what's going on?"

"I—I'm sorry, I had to lie to get you here. I didn't think you'd come if you knew the truth."

"The truth? What is the truth?" Harper asked, pulling away from him.

"The truth is that... I love you. I love you and...the cameras in our house weren't put there by the Fullers."

"They weren't?"

"They were put there by me," he said, placing his face in his hands. "I had my student order them, and I got caught." He shrugged, as if it were no big deal.

She took a breath. "I don't understand..."

He shook his head, his forehead wrinkled as he lifted his head to meet her eyes. "I don't know why I did it. I just…I felt guilty, I guess. I wanted to make us leave. I wanted you to understand that it wasn't my fault. We needed to leave Lancaster Mills, and the only way I could make that happen was to scare you. I'm so, so sorry. I'm an idiot." He reached for her hands through the bars, but she stepped back.

"So, wait…you mean to tell me that the cameras—the ones I've been having nightmares about, the ones that have caused me to be so paranoid—that was all you?"

He nodded, poking out his lips in a pout. "I'm so sorry."

"What about everything else? The appointments? The slashed tires? Tori's bra?"

"You were right when you said you thought I'd been the one to leave the house last when we went to Myrtle Beach. I left it open on purpose. Just slightly. Remember I went back in to grab a drink? I hung Tori's bra up on the chair. I used an excuse to sneak into her house when the housekeeper was home alone and took it."

"But…she said it was her. Why would she cover for you?"

"I don't know," he said honestly. "That threw me off, too. I guess she was just trying to help, but she was holding everything we'd done over me. So, I tried to confess with the pizzas. I wanted you to confront me…but then I couldn't go through with it. I was so scared I was going to lose you."

"The mugging, then? You were never really mugged, were you? That was all you? Do you know how many nights I stayed up driving myself crazy about it happening again? Worrying about who had our key? What about the tires? You really slashed your own tires?"

"I was an idiot," he said. "I needed to get your attention. I needed you to know we were both in danger."

"*But we weren't both in danger,*" she squealed, hot, angry tears cascading down her cheeks. "How could you do this?

All of it...the abortion appointments, too? Those were made before you even knew I was pregnant."

He looked down, rubbing his fingers across his forehead. "I listened to your voicemail when you were in the shower. You had a missed call, and I didn't recognize the number."

"So, what? You thought I might be cheating on you for a change?" she demanded, fury radiating through her.

"It was your nurse, calling to let you know they'd called in a prenatal for you. I put it all together at that point."

"And you...you got me fired?"

He nodded. "I needed you to need me, Harper. I needed it to be me and you against the world, like it's always been."

"The lingerie? The mail? All of it?"

"It was all me," he said sadly. "All of it. Because I'd screwed up and I couldn't face it. I wanted you to believe we were both in danger, so I did everything I could to make you want us to leave. Only...you wanted to leave alone. So I tried to scare you even more. I couldn't let you leave without me. I can't survive without you."

She let out a sob, trying hard to control her overwhelming emotions as she thought back over the past few weeks. How could what he was saying be true? "What about the email from Donna? You said she said the neighbors freaked her out. I saw the email myself."

He exhaled deeply, looking away. "I sent the email. I really did email Donna, in case she had something bad to say about them that would back up all I was trying to prove. But, she didn't email back. So, I created an email and sent it to myself." He paused. "Then I emailed back with the kind of response I was hoping for."

"What about the article that went missing? You weren't even home then."

"That was just...lucky coincidence. I found the article a few days later on the floor. I guess it had fallen off the desk. We were just so panicked we didn't think to look for it."

"*I,*" she corrected. "*I* was just so panicked. Because it was all just an act for you." When he didn't respond, she spoke up again. "So, literally all of it…all of it was…just a *game*? You just played mind games with me and let me live in terror for the past few weeks for no reason? The neighbors weren't really bad at all?"

"Well, they weren't *good.* They were obviously trying to cause problems and break us up."

She shook her head, backing away from him. "And you could've resisted, Bryant. Just like I did. They didn't deserve to have their lives ruined because of us."

"I didn't start the fire," he assured her. "I swear to you I had nothing to do with that."

"How could you do this?" She begged him for an explanation that wouldn't make her hate him more, her lips curled in disgust.

"I don't know. I'm just so sorry. I don't know how to fix it, but I'm trying. I could still lie to you. They're dead; I could let them take the blame. But I'm not. I'm telling you the truth now. About everything," he said. "I want to be completely honest, so we can fix this. Ask me anything you want. This," he pointed around the jail cell, "was a wake up call, Harper. I'm never going to let a lie come between us again."

She closed her eyes, trying to collect her thoughts. "You don't honestly believe we're going to be okay, now, do you? You lied to me…about everything. You cheated on me. You ruined peoples' lives. You ruined *my* life. You were going to let me hire a lawyer. Waste my parents money when you truly are guilty."

He shook his head, looking at the guard at the far side of the room. "They charged me with filing a false police report. It's a misdemeanor. I already told them everything I'm telling you. I'm cooperating fully. No more lies. What I did...it was wrong. I realize that now. But it's not too late to fix what's still important to me. I'll get a fine, maybe community service, but no jail time. A lawyer can help. I still need one."

She stared at him, at the man she thought she knew, but he seemed to be a stranger. A monster. A man who'd done unspeakable things just to get his way—just to protect himself from his own lies. She couldn't deny that she still loved him, but that love was overshadowed by disgust. How could she try to help him after all he'd done? How could she try to work it out?

The truth was, she couldn't. She rested her hand on her belly, on the child she was going to raise to be nothing like the man who'd fathered him or her.

"I have to go," she said finally, brushing tears from her cheeks.

"What?" He pulled his head back from the cell's bars in shock. "What are you talking about?"

"I can't be here right now," she said, taking a step back. "I'm going back to Chicago. I gave up everything for you. I gave up a career I worked my ass off for in college. I was willing to start entry-level and work my way up rather than use my degree just so you could do what you love. And you were so grateful that you cheated on me. Then you lied about it over and over again. About everything. I can't do this anymore. I'm going home. When you get all of this sorted out, we can figure out custody. We can do whatever we need to in order to make sure our child has a good life, but whatever we had...between us...it's over. It burned down right along with the Fullers' house. What you did...it wasn't to protect me. It was to protect yourself." She paused. "And now I have to do the same."

"Don't do this," he whispered, tears filling his eyes. "You can't leave me. I love you."

She nodded, but turned away, walking back down the hallway and ignoring his cries. There was nothing left to say. She wouldn't pack a bag; there was nothing here she needed to take. She was going home, to start over and try to forget about the nightmare the months in Lancaster Mills had brought her.

CHAPTER FIFTY-FOUR

HARPER

FOUR YEARS LATER

Harper sat at a prime table in a prestigious restaurant across from the CEO of Chicago's top hospital and two of his assistants. He slid a piece of paper across the table, taking a sip of his wine and smiling.

"I think you'll find that it's more than we had originally discussed. After talking with your references, it's important to me that you know how big of an asset you'd be to our hospital."

She smiled, staring at the paper. The number was double what she made in a year where she currently worked. It was enough to pay off her lawyer's bill from the custody case with Bryant. It was enough to pay for Luke's school. Enough to pay off her house within a few years. Enough to take care of her for life. She set the paper down, trying not to let tears flood her eyes as she pictured the future she'd always dreamed of with her son by her side in the city she loved more than anything.

"It's…yes," she said simply. "I would love to accept."

The CEO clapped his hands. "Now, that's exactly what I had hoped for. More wine for the table to celebrate this new endeavor." He waved to a nearby waiter who jumped to action, bringing a new bottle of wine instantly.

"Thank you so much," she said, reaching out and shaking her new employer's hand. "I hope you'll understand if I need to go, though. My daycare will be closing soon," she checked her watch, "and I need to pick up my son."

"Of course," he said politely. "We'll see you in two weeks?"

"Two weeks," she confirmed, shaking his hand and the hands of his assistants once more as she lifted the napkin from her lap and set it on the table. "Thank you so much again for this amazing opportunity."

"We look forward to having you," he said sincerely. She stood, walking away from the table with a chest full of exuberant joy. It was all she could do not to break out in dance right there in the restaurant. As soon as she was out of their line of vision, she began walking quicker, bustling through the busy restaurant on her way toward the door. Luke's school was open for another hour, but she wanted to celebrate the good news with him. In the past four years, her amazing son had become her best friend. Bryant came around on the weekends—*sometimes*—but he'd taken a job two states away, so his involvement had been minimal. She had an incredible job, and incredible son, and an incredible life since she'd left Lancaster Mills, and in a way, it was all thanks to her ex-husband. He'd shown her his true colors in enough time for her to save herself from years of heartbreak, something many women weren't lucky enough to have.

She *was* lucky, though some days it was harder to see than others. Today was not one of those days. Today was perfect— her thoughts were interrupted as she ran straight into a restaurant patron.

"I'm so sorry," she said, reaching out a hand to touch his

arm. He'd been bent over, picking something up off the floor, and she'd missed him, running straight into him and knocking him over. He looked up at her and her gasp caught in her throat. "I'm..."

He stood, his expression just as shocked as she felt. It had been four years since she'd seen Jason Fuller, the dark eyes that caused her stomach to do backflips and the smile that warmed the darkest parts of her soul. "Hi," he said politely, reaching out a hand. "I'm Nathan."

She stared at him, wondering for a moment if she were wrong about who she'd thought he was, but his wink caused her to smile back. She took his hand, their skin colliding with electricity. She didn't dare let go. "Hi, Nathan, I'm Harper."

"Harper," he said her name slowly. "It's...*great* to meet you."

She tucked a piece of hair behind her ear, her face warming under his stare. "You too."

"Can I buy you a drink?" he asked, looking at the table he'd been at. It was filled with five guys who were around Jas —*Nathan's* age and watching them as if they were an episode of television. "You guys minds if I duck out?"

"Go right ahead," one of the men said, his tone heavy with innuendo.

"I'm sorry," Harper said. "I mean, thank you for the invitation. I have to go pick up my son."

Nathan nodded, his happiness fading quickly. "Oh, okay, of course."

She smiled at him one last time, tucking her purse back over her arm as she went to walk away. "It was...really nice to see you."

The smile he gave her in return was sad but polite. "You too, Harper." He took a drink of his beer as she walked past him. After a few steps, she turned around.

"Nathan?"

He spun on his heel to face her. "Yeah?"

"How long are you in town?"

"Oh," he said, obviously caught off guard. "I live here now. I work for the paper."

Her heart raced. He was close. In the same city. At the same stoplights and restaurants. Caught in the same traffic jams. It was her chance. A chance she never thought she'd have again. "Would you like to have dinner with me tomorrow night?" she offered, adrenaline coursing through her.

His eyes widened just a bit as shock filled his face, but his expression warmed quickly. "I would love that," he said.

"Good," she told him. "Me too."

She reached out to take his hand one last time, desperate for his touch, and he kissed the back of her hand. "Until tomorrow," he whispered, and it was like they were the only people in the room. Everything else silenced as she stared into the eyes she'd dreamed about weekly for the past four years. The eyes she never thought she'd see again.

Before she realized what was happening, his arms were around her waist, his lips on hers in a passionate embrace. It was fast, too fast for a single mom, and yet not fast enough for the woman who'd dreamed of this exact thing happening for so long. He smelled the same, his touch felt the same, and yet everything had changed. The biggest change: that she was single now. That she could enjoy this now. That she could live in the moment with him. That this was a possibility. Not just a possibility…a reality. He pulled away from her, his lips red from their kiss, and she was vaguely aware of the men he'd been dining with snickering. But it didn't matter. Nothing mattered. He was here—no longer a figment of her daydreams—and there were no more secrets between them, only freedom. Freedom to build a new life. One they'd both started on four years ago.

Lancaster Mills had taken so much from her, but as she released his hands, their eyes still locked together, she realized how much it had given her, too.

"I'll meet you here tomorrow at six?" he asked.

"Sounds good," she told him, still in a slight daze. *Good.* For the first time in so long, everything about her life was good.

DON'T MISS THE NEXT PSYCHOLOGICAL THRILLER FROM KIERSTEN MODGLIN

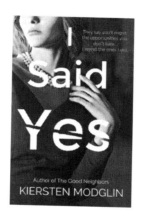

They had the perfect marriage until the cracks began to show. Who is lying in this twisted domestic suspense? Better question: who isn't?

Read *I Said Yes* today:
https://amzn.to/30XX1gv

DON'T MISS THE NEXT KIERSTEN MODGLIN RELEASE!

Thank you so much for reading this story. I'd love to invite you to sign up for my mailing list and text alerts so we can be sure you don't miss my next release.

Sign up for my mailing list here:
http://eepurl.com/dhiRRv
Sign up for my text alerts here:
www.kierstenmodglinauthor.com/textalerts.html

ENJOYED THE GOOD NEIGHBORS?

If you enjoyed this story, please consider leaving me a quick review. It doesn't have to be long—just a few words will do. Who knows? Your review might be the thing that encourages a future reader to take a chance on my work!
To leave a review, please visit:
https://www.amazon.com/dp/B07RPKLSX3

Check out The Good Neighbors on Goodreads:
https://www.goodreads.com/book/show/45728541-the-good-neighbors

ACKNOWLEDGMENTS

When I first began writing The Good Neighbors (at the time it was titled Don't Wake the Neighbors), I wasn't sure I was ever going to be able to finish it. Honestly, it scared me too much. It's a very real fear, isn't it?

The idea for this story came to me when my husband and I were shopping for our first house. A coworker of mine was having a horrible time with her neighbors and her stories began to terrify me as we shopped for our own home. I worried...what if our neighbors are terrible, too? Growing up in the middle of nowhere with no one around, the idea of living next door to someone I didn't get along with for the rest of my life (or the foreseeable future, at least) was enough to cause me severe nightmares.

I'm happy to report our new neighbors have been wonderful, but I'm also forever grateful for that fear because it culminated in this chilling story idea: what if the new neighbors weren't good at all?

Although the people I need to thank for helping me with this story aren't *literally* my neighbors, they are a part of my inner circle—my community, if you will—and I couldn't do any of this without them.

To *my husband, Michael, and my daughter, CB*—thank you for loving me through all of my writer's block, crazy moments, insane deadlines, and sleep-deprived states. I love the two of you more than you could ever possibly understand. Without you, none of this would be possible.

To *my family—my parents, sisters, grandparents, aunts, uncles, and cousins—*thank you for being such a huge part of who I am. Thank you for the lessons you've taught me, the stories you've shared, and the support you've given. Without you, I was just a little girl who may never have believed in herself enough to give this a shot. I love you.

To *Emerald O'Brien, Rachel Renee, and Lauren Lee—*my suspenseful sisters. I'm so incredibly thankful to have you ladies on this journey with me. Thank you for your advice when I'm struggling, your willingness to listen when I need to vent, and your unwavering support in everything I do. I can't wait to see where this beautiful journey takes us and I'm glad we're in it together.

To *my amazing editor, Sarah West—*I've said it before and I'll say it again, you are an absolute super star! The things you manage to catch, your insight, and your dedication to my books and characters is unmatched. I'm forever thankful that we crossed paths.

To *my wonderful proofreader, Lyssa Dawn—*thank you for being my last set of eyes. I'm so grateful for your attention to detail and love of great stories.

To *my Twisted Readers, Street Team, and Review Team—*you guys are everything to me. I couldn't do this without your support. On a rough day, I can always turn to my groups to make me laugh or encourage me to keep going. Most of you have been here since the beginning and I love you all so much! Thank you for giving me the inspiration for some of the crazy pranks that took place in this story.

To *my beta readers, Emerald, Brittany, Rachel, and Dawn—*thank you for being my first words of encouragement when I was sure this book was utter crap. This book is 1000x better thanks to your advice, insight, and questions. Thank you for believing in these characters and pushing me to be better.

And, lastly, to *you—*thank you for purchasing this book

and supporting art. Thank you for being a reader. Thank you for every review, every recommendation, every share on social media. Thank you, most of all, for making my dreams come true. Without you, I would just be a girl with a head full of stories and no one to share them with.

ABOUT THE AUTHOR

Kiersten Modglin is an Amazon Top 30 bestselling author of psychological thrillers, a member of International Thriller Writers and the Alliance of Independent Authors, a KDP Select All-Star, and a ThrillerFix Best Psychological Thriller Award Recipient. Kiersten grew up in rural Western Kentucky with dreams of someday publishing a book or two. With more than twenty-five books published to date, Kiersten now lives in Nashville, Tennessee with her husband, daughter, and their two Boston Terriers: Cedric and Georgie. She is best known for her unpredictable psychological suspense. Kiersten's work is currently being translated into multiple languages and readers across the world refer to her as 'The Queen of Twists.' A Netflix addict, Shonda Rhimes super-fan, psychology fanatic, and indoor enthusiast, Kiersten enjoys rainy days spent with her nose in a book.

Sign up for Kiersten's newsletter here:
http://eepurl.com/b3cNFP
Sign up for text alerts from Kiersten here:
www.kierstenmodglinauthor.com/textalerts.html

www.kierstenmodglinauthor.com
www.facebook.com/kierstenmodglinauthor
www.facebook.com/groups/kmodsquad
www.twitter.com/kmodglinauthor
www.instagram.com/kierstenmodglinauthor
www.tiktok.com/@kierstenmodglinauthor
www.goodreads.com/kierstenmodglinauthor
www.bookbub.com/authors/kiersten-modglin
www.amazon.com/author/kierstenmodglin

ALSO BY KIERSTEN MODGLIN

The Liar (The Messes, #3)

The Prisoner (The Messes, #4)

NOVELLAS

The Long Route: A Lover's Landing Novella

The Stranger in the Woods: A Crimson Falls Novella

THE LOCKE INDUSTRIES NOVELS

The Nanny's Secret

Made in the USA
Las Vegas, NV
27 January 2025

17042491R00143